American Bad Boy

American Bad Boy

A Military Romance

EDDIE CLEVELAND

If you're looking for billionaires or shifters, you won't find them here. Eddie writes what he knows: bad boys, hot sex and crazy love.

CHAPTER 1:

Year–2004

Lauren

"Hey-yah!"

"Shake it like a polaroid picture!" we cheer in unison.

Surrounded by a circle of my closest friends, breaking it down in gowns that are preparing us for future bridesmaid duty. I can't believe how much fun I'm having. I look over at Becky and she's shaking her little money maker in wild abandon. She's in her glory right now. After months of us trying to derail her visions for our prom night theme, it finally came together. And, I've got to admit, it looks spectacular.

When she first started pushing for a "Fairy-tale" theme at the council meetings, I rolled my eyes harder than anyone else. In all fairness though, her first pitch really wasn't the best. Thankfully, we did manage to evolve her Disney princess idea from one that gave me a horrible flashback of my childhood fear of Mickey Mouse into the stunning setting we are dancing in now. The white, silver and teal blue balloons are tied in clusters and hung from the ceiling to look like magical clouds. At least they do under this low light. And the miles of silky fabric hung around the room transformed the Colorado Golf Club into a dreamlike stage for the class of 2004 to dance the night away in.

It feels like everything came together tonight so perfectly, it might as well be a fairytale. Just a week ago, I was crying in my doctor's office over an ear infection that had me so dizzy I was convinced I'd never make it to the prom tonight, let alone dance at it. I sobbed like a four-year-old lost in a department store when Dr. Klebes confirmed that I would need a day off from school and a round of antibiotics to get it under control.

"But, but, my prom! My dress! I can't be sick. I can't miss it!" I'm not proud to say I cried real tears. He told me that I'd be fine by tonight, if I just got plenty of rest, water and took the pills. Turns out, he knew what he was talking about and my mini-meltdown was for nothing.

I guess all those degrees on his wall meant something after all.

As OutKast fades out, my girls and I all stand around and stare blankly at each other as we wait for the next song to tell us what to do. Will it be another fast one? Should we stay in our little scrum of ruffles and sequins? Or is the tempo change gonna send us searching for the guys we showed up with?

Beauty queen of only eighteen
She had some trouble with herself

We quickly stampede off the floor in different directions as Adam Levine begins to serenade us. It doesn't take long to spot Mack, he's exactly where I left him three songs ago. Luckily for me, he looks just as sexy as he did three songs ago too. I navigate through the obstacle course of tables and chairs until I reach the back wall he's leaning against. If I didn't know better, I'd think he was hiding.

Unfortunately, for him, he's not hard to spot. Hovering around six feet tall, with chiseled shoulders that even his tux jacket can't hide, he can't exactly covertly disappear behind a plant in the corner or something. Mack has a face that makes every girl in the room melt and a body that they all wish they could lay beside. It used to make me jealous, all the attention he gets, but he's never cared about anyone but me. It's been that way since we were kids and it'll be that way until we're old. Besides, everyone knows that Mack's taken. They can take their chances with Cameron Armstrong instead.

As the quarterback of our high school football team, Cameron's never had a problem getting attention from the girls. With his sandy brown hair and deep blue eyes, the fact that he's the second best looking guy in the school doesn't hurt either. I'd give him a second look, if I wasn't already with the best looking guy. And if he wasn't a non-committal manwhore.

Mack's eyes light up when he sees me, like I just woke him from a dream. I love when he looks at me like that. If there were other girls in the room, you wouldn't know it by the way he smiles at me. It's like I'm the only woman in the world, let alone in the dance hall.

"C'mon. It's your turn to dance with me," I tug on both of his hands and try to pull him off the wall. "Just dance one slow song with me and then I won't bug you anymore." I plead.

"Nah, I'm gonna sit this one out." He doesn't budge an inch. I could throw every ounce of strength I have into trying to move him, but it wouldn't matter. He's built like a stack of bricks. Hard, cut, strong bricks that have made every girl jealous of me since we started going out.

"Just one song." I persist, still pulling feebly on his hands. He won't give in. I know he won't. "Why did you ask me to come to the prom with you if you weren't gonna dance?" I stick out my bottom lip in a pouty face that I hope will sway him. "I spent weeks picking out this dress, I'm never gonna look this good again. I don't want to waste the night standing by the wall."

He doesn't need to know that by weeks I mean months. As in, I've been planning what to wear to the prom since school started this year. I smooth my hands down over my royal purple gown. After looking at every neon colored dress ever invented, I turned down the flash for understated elegance. I truly feel like a princess with the intricately beaded halter and the floor length chiffon skirt. All that's missing is my glass slippers.

That and my prince charming.

Mack Forrester is many things. Usually words like "hot" and "rebel" are used to describe him. But he isn't a prince, and the only thing he's good at charming is my clothes off.

And she will be loved …

"The song is almost over. Just dance with me for a minute. Just till the end of the song." I try again. Mack just smiles at me and tilts his head to the side.

"You do look gorgeous," his voice rumbles. "But, I didn't come here to dance. I brought you because I knew it was important to you." He pushes himself off the wall and stands up straight, lifting my hand up over my head and twirls me in a circle. I squint my eyes and the room swirls around me in a kaleidoscope of color. My dress billows out, exposing my legs to the air, and then cocoons back around me. I feel like the tiny ballerina I used to watch spin around in my mother's music box.

No one would dance with her either.

Mack yanks me tight against his chest and fixes me to the floor with his blue eyes. "Besides, there's a lot more to do on prom night than just this," he nods his head toward the swaying couples behind me. "I *do* plan to dance with you," he smirks his cocky little half smile and my heart flutters. I'm sure he can feel it thudding in my chest. "Don't worry, I'll spin you all around too, but for *my* dance that pretty little dress of yours has got to go."

I don't mean to press my breasts into him. It's not like I want to encourage him. I just can't help it. Mack knows how to mesmerize me with only a look. The song changes to another slow one and I manage to snap out of my lust trance.

"Fine, if you're not going to dance with me then I'll just find someone else who will." I look into his eyes and fight my instinct to kiss his hovering mouth.

"Who? Why are we wasting time here? Let's just get out of here, Lauren." His voice is thick with desire. I can almost feel myself being hypnotized by it. But I refuse to give in that easy.

Somehow I find the strength to step away from his warm body and scan the room. My eyes stop on Joel Brickman. Not ideal by a long stretch, but I know my former chemistry partner won't turn down a dance. I smirk at Mack and walk away from him, making sure I add a little Shakira to my hips as I make my way across the floor. I know Mack's watching my every move, so I might as well put on a good show.

I stride up to Joel and grab his arm. "Come on, let's dance."

It isn't a question. But, it doesn't seem to matter. He's at my heels like the love-struck puppy dog he is.

We're quickly absorbed on the ballroom floor by the other couples twisting around in slow circles. I glance at Joel and am rewarded with the familiar smile I've seen for the past eight months in every science class. His look says I've just made this guy's night. Hell, I probably just made his year. I check over his shoulder to see if Mack is watching and feel satisfied when my boyfriend's smug smile begins to twist into something else. Jealousy.

Some people want diamond rings
Some just want everything
But everything means nothing
If I ain't got you, yeah

Joel glides me around the floor and my view of Mack is obstructed by other slow-dancing couples. I finally stop twisting my head around like an owl and just focus on the guy I'm dancing with. His large brown eyes are searching my face. Desperate to find significance in our meaningless dance. I've sat next to him all year, yet I've never really looked at him before. He's actually not a bad looking guy. His sandy hair sweeps across his forehead and frames his big eyes. The eyes that won't stop staring at me.

Staring into me.

I need to make him stop.

"I, uh, wanted to say thanks for being my lab partner all year. It was great working with you." I interrupt his thoughts in an attempt to drag him back into reality. I can't look into those eyes any longer. Instead I focus on my hand against his shoulder. My almond skin against his snow white jacket is striking.

"I can honestly say that it was my pleasure, Lauren. Did you get into nursing?" He looks so hopeful, like my future genuinely matters to him.

"I did," I beam. I can't help it, I'm pretty proud of myself. "I got a full scholarship at the University of Colorado, can you believe it?"

"Of course."

I suddenly realize that I have zero idea of what Joel's plans are after graduation. I've talked to him almost every day this school year, but now that I think about it, I can't recall any of the details he's told me about his life. At all. A flash of guilt washes over me.

"Are you going to university?" I ask shyly. I can't believe how self-centered I've been. My mind is struggling to come up with one thing I know about this guy other than the fact that he's good at science and crushing on me hard. I'm coming up blank.

If he's offended, it doesn't show. "I did. I'll be at Colorado U too. I got into the engineering program."

"Oh, congrats." I feel like a jerk for not knowing that. But not enough of a jerk to stop searching over his shoulder for my boyfriend. When I've rotated back around enough that Mack's back in clear view, I can see he doesn't look impressed.

Good. Serves him right for refusing to dance with me. I smile to myself.

Some just want everything
But everything means nothing
If I ain't got you, yeah.

I see Mack pushing his way through the tables and chairs until he's no longer in view. The song is almost over and this time when I spot Mack he's at the edge of the dance floor. The last note is being sung as he springs toward me like a tiger from the bushes.

"Thanks for the dance, Joel." I smile and step back. I thud right into the human pillar that is my boyfriend. I feel his arms wrap around my body as he pulls me against him possessively.

"All right, you've made your point. Let's get out of here." he hisses in my ear.

Joel looks at me, then over my shoulder, smiling politely. "Thank you for the dance, Lauren. I'll see you on campus next year." He gives my hand a quick squeeze before dropping it back to my side. Before I even have a chance to respond, I'm being guided toward the exit with a sense of urgency.

I don't bother looking back over my shoulder as we leave. There's no point. My future is with Mack.

Scratch that.

My future *is* Mack. And nostalgia has no place in his plans.

CHAPTER 2:

Year–2004

Lauren

"Where are we going?" I allow him to guide me through the front doors and into the night air. Instead of walking toward the valet parking, he tightens his grip on my hand and leads me down the side of the building behind the hedges.

Mack stops and turns around quickly, almost knocking me off balance. Luckily, his hand steadies me before I have a chance to twist an ankle in these heels. I don't know why I ever let my sister,

Chelsea, talk me into wearing them. I'm the kind of girl who practically gets vertigo from a quarter-inch heel on my flats.

I balked at the 6-inch heels she originally campaigned for. *"I'm not a stripper! I'll break my damned neck in those."* I pushed the crushed velvet shoes back into her arms. She wrinkled her nose at me and gave me that look she always gives me when she thinks I'm still acting like a baby. I *hate* that look. I hate it so much that I'm teetering on 4-inch heels on the lawn of the Colorado golf club, trying not to snap my ankles.

Thoughts of Chelsea's "helpful" fashion choices flit away as soon as I look into Mack's crystal blue eyes. Even now, after twelve years of looking into them, I'm unable to look away. That color, it unnerves me and soothes me at the same time. They're like waves crashing against a Hawaiian beach, if you could only manage to stay on the sand and listen, you'd be captivated by their tranquility. But instead, you find yourself trying to surf them, obsessed with the idea of taming them, knowing full well the danger that lurks beneath.

He leans into me, his frame pressed up hard against mine, and I let out a small sigh. When his soft lips find mine, my eyelids flutter closed. The thudding bass from the dance hall is drowned out by my own heartbeat. When he steps back, it takes me a second to stop making a fishy face at the night air, my lips still desperately trying to kiss a ghost.

My eyes snap open and this time all I can see in Mack's eyes is lust. I look over my shoulder, we're barely ten feet away from the front door. These cedar hedges would've been an awesome fort hide out when we were kids, but they aren't doing much to hide us as adults.

"Mack, if you think we're gonna mess around here ... there's no way." My voice is a strained whisper.

"Oh come on, Lauren. You think I'm gonna try something here?" He pretends to be offended.

I *do*, actually.

If I know anything about Mack, and I know a lot, it's that he would try to have sex with me anywhere.

Any place.

Any time.

God, I thought that I was helping him gain some maturity and restraint when I insisted we wait until my eighteenth. If anything, I think all that waiting turned him into an animal. Not that I'm complaining.

"I just wanted to kiss you. No funny business," he puts his hands up in surrender. "Jeez, what kind of perv are you anyway? Thinking about getting naked in the bushes? I always knew you were a wild one," he smirks.

Heat rises in my cheeks and I tilt my head away. I don't want him to see it written all over my face how much the idea really does excite me.

"Well, what are we doing then?"

"You'll see." His eyes twinkle brighter than the stars above us and for just a moment, I wonder if I should go back on my "no-sex-in-the-hedges" policy. He weaves his fingers in mine and steadies me by holding my arm with his other hand as he leads the way around the country club. The light gets dimmer as we sneak around the building to the back until we're stumbling through the darkness toward a garage.

What the?

"Ok, just wait here a sec. I'll be less than a minute. I promise." He stifles my questions with a quick kiss before he quickly jogs over the grass to the shadows.

I squint to watch him approach the garage. Out from the side door pops a young man who Mack clearly knows. They look like old buds, clapping each other's shoulders and laughing. I watch Mack dig out his wallet and give the guy a couple bills and then his buddy disappears back inside. Is he getting drugs? No, that's not like Mack. Some booze? More likely, but I don't know why he'd have to get it back here. There'll be tons of drinks at the after party.

I watch as Mack waits by the door and listen to the crickets in the distance, punctuating the night air. The serenity is short lived as a grinding noise fills my ears. The large garage door slides up loudly as white light spills out into the darkness. Inside are rows of golf carts lined up like little soldiers.

The guy steers one of the carts out the front door and comes to a jerky stop by my boyfriend. I watch as they shake hands again and then Mack jumps in the cart and drives out over the grass toward me as the garage door slinks back down, keeping his transaction a secret. His cocky smile is pasted in place as he pulls up beside me. I can't help but return it.

"Hop in," he pats the empty seat next to him casually. Like he's not breaking a bunch of laws right now. Like we're gonna go putt on the green and have a few rounds of golf.

I'm sure there will be a few rounds involved, I'll even get to practice my long and short stroke.

How can a girl resist?

CHAPTER 3:

Year-2004

Lauren

I climb into the cart. As soon as I have my dress tucked in around my legs, Mack is speeding up across the green.

"Whoa, slow down. I don't want you to flip this thing!" I clutch the bar over my head for stability.

"Relax, you know I've got you."

I *do* know.

I know he's looked after me since I was six years old and fell off my Rainbow Brite bike. He wiped the tiny pebbles from my skinned knees and the tears from my eyes. I can't even count how many times he's soothed away my fears or sadness since that day. I can't imagine how many more times he will in our future. Mack wraps his arm around my shoulder and I drop my head against him, breathing in his scent. Where ever we're going, I know I'm safe in his arms.

He drives us up a fairly steep slope and I listen to the night air rush by us. If I listen close enough, I can almost hear our story on the wind. Our history being played out and our destiny unfolding. I can almost hear the songs and laughter of our childhood being erased by the loving murmurs of our years to come.

Mack reaches the top of the hill and parks the cart. He slides out onto the green and pulls a blanket out from behind the seat. He smoothly spreads it out over the grass with a flick of his wrist before walking over to me and extending his hand to help me out of the cart.

Kicking my heels off, I step out onto the cool grass. Once we reach the blanket, I notice I can see the reflection of the moon and stars in a small lake below.

"It's beautiful!"

"That lake looks like a swamp compared to you." he answers, his voice low. He walks up behind me and slips his arms around me. His lips quickly find their way to that tender spot on my neck that he knows drives me crazy. I remember back in seventh grade when

Mack left a hickey on that spot. Mom wasn't impressed. I smile at the memory and close my eyes as tingles of desire prickle along my skin.

He cups his hand against my cheek and guides my mouth back to his, our tongues dance against each other to a song only they can hear. Mack pushes his body tight against mine and I lean back against him, instinctively grinding my ass back against his hardening cock. Butterflies erupt in a frenzied flight inside my chest just from feeling his excitement through our clothes. We've only been having sex for a couple months now, so each time is still new and naughty. I hope the thrill never goes away.

I turn around to face him, eager to look into his eyes. To see his face when he undresses me. His pink lips hover over mine, the heat of his breath billows over my cheek, making the warm night feel frosty in comparison. Mack's fingers trail down over my face as he looks into me, like he's lost in us. In more than this moment. In more than the sex. In all of us. His eyes flit back into focus and he presses his lips down against mine in a bruising kiss.

His hands find my zipper and make quick work of tugging it down far enough that my breasts are exposed to the night. Mack flutters soft kisses down my neck and across my collar bone. My stomach twists up tight in anticipation of his wet mouth finding it's way to my nipple. When at last he does, I throw my head back and look up at the bright moon as small ripples of pleasure radiate through me. With my arms laced around his neck, I'm practically hanging off of him while he kisses my nipple, licking around it and then flickering his tongue over it. The air feels icy against it as he abandons my left nipple for my right and I arch my back hungrily, hoping he'll never stop.

Slick desire is blossoming between my legs and spreading to my panties. As his tongue twists and teases my nipples, I cry out to the stars, surprised by my own voice. Mack stops and looks down at me, his smirk ever present.

"Sorry, that was kinda loud." I look down.

"Mmmm, I like it," he teases. "Let's see if I can get you to *really* make some noise."

He pulls me down to the blanket and tugs my dress down over my body as I wriggle to be freed from it impatiently. Once he has it pulled down over my ankles, he tosses the gown beside us on the grass, like an afterthought. Normally, lying under him in nothing but my lacey underwear while he's still fully dressed would make me feel self-conscious. But tonight, with the moon and stars as our light combined with the way he's looking at me make me lean up on my elbows and tilt my head to the side, happy to let him look.

"God, Lauren, you're so beautiful." His voice is hoarse.

"Thank you," I whisper back. "How about letting me see you?" I let my eyes trail down over his tuxedo and feel those butterflies beating their wings again at the idea of him stripping it off.

"You don't need to ask me twice." He slides his coat off onto the ground in a pile. The rest of his clothes are quick to follow making a small mountain of fabric next to us. His cut muscles challenge my eyes to focus on just one place.

He leans over me and his warm fingers slide under the edge of my panties, hooking them and pulling until he's tugged them off me. I sit up a bit and dip my fingers under the waistband of his underwear. I still feel shy about undressing him. I slowly pull them down until his cock is exposed and wobbling in front of my face. I can't help but gasp. I try to wrap my fingers around it, desperate to feel him, but Mack softly pushes me back against the blanket.

"I want you, Lauren. I need to be in you." He lowers himself onto me and braces himself with a strong arm on each side of my body. My eyes are drawn to the definition in his bicep, then the blue of his eyes. "Are you ready?" he murmurs.

I nod and bite my lip as he presses the head of his cock against my slick opening. He pushes himself into me and I can feel my body opening around his thick shaft. Even though this isn't our first time, it still stings a little when he thrusts his hips and fully buries his member inside me. I wrap my arms back around his neck. The need to feel his skin pressed against mine is overwhelming. The way his frame covers me is soothing, like a warm blanket in a thunder storm.

Mack inches his cock into me, until his hips are flush with the insides of my thighs. I open my legs further, twisting my feet around the backs of his knees, allowing him to fill me even more. When he pulls back and pumps into me again, I gasp at the tiny pinch of pain giving way to pleasure. Mack thrusts into me and I tilt my hips up to him, trying to feel him inside me as deeply as I can.

He drops his head down and pulls my nipple into his mouth, sucking on it hard. I swear I see stars and it isn't the ones in the sky. Warmth grows in my belly as his cock slides inside me. Little waves of ecstasy ripple through me as our bodies perfectly fit together. His breaths are quickening and his movements are getting jerky when a tidal wave of pressure and bliss crash down on me, leaving me screaming Mack's name into the darkness. I can feel his cum filling me up inside as he grinds down against me, his hips shuddering against my thighs.

We don't move. We just lie here and listen to the night and our breathing. The crickets are back, I suppose they never left, but I can hear them again. Singing for us. I'd like to think of it as applause. Mack pulls back from me and a little bit of his seed spills onto the blanket. I don't care. That's what the pill is for. It's not like he's some kind of manwhore. We are each other's first and last.

"I told you I could make you even noisier," he puffs out his chest proudly. He was right. For once I'm not even embarrassed.

"That felt amazing." I don't tell him that it's the first time I've ever had an orgasm from sex. I don't want to bruise his ego.

"You're amazing," he pulls me toward him, lying back on the blanket and holding me in his arms. We stare at the night sky together, neither of us in a hurry to get dressed. I feel like I could lay in his arms like this forever. At least until dawn. The early morning golfers might have an issue with forever.

"I can't believe that this is the end. The end and the beginning. I really feel like we're starting a new chapter together, you know?"

I ramble, breathing in the sweet smell of fresh cut grass and his cologne. He doesn't answer me; I hope he's not falling asleep.

"You know what though? I can't wait for all the chapters," I continue. "I can't wait for us to buy our first janky futon together and for us to buy grocery carts of ramen noodles. I can't wait for when we get married, you know, after college I mean. And when we start having kids together. I think two kids is good, what do you think? I'm even looking forward to when we get all old and hunched over together," I smile at the sky.

Nothing. Just Mack breathing. Oh, jeez, he did fall asleep.

"Mack?"

"Yeah."

Or not.

"Why aren't you saying anything?"

Those crickets sound even louder. Less like they're applauding now and more like they're mocking me.

"Mack?"

Crap. I probably freaked him out with my sixty-year forecast into the future. "Hey, you know I'm just talking right? I don't really have big plans for that far away …"

"Lauren, I need to tell you something."

Double crap.

He sits up and I sit next to him. His eyebrows are knit together and his mouth is twisted to the side. "What's going on? Did I freak you out about the future?"

"No, it's not that."

"Then what?"

"Lauren, I got into West Point."

"West Point? The military academy? But you didn't even tell me you were applying? In New York? What about my scholarship? What about our plans? When are you going?" My mouth rattles off the questions as quickly as my mind can form them.

Mack looks down at his hands, then into my eyes. "I'm leaving in three days."

CHAPTER 4:

Year–2004

Lauren

"Three days?" I squeak.

I'm searching his face for signs that this is a badly timed joke. There's no twinkle in his eyes like when he mixed mustard with frosting and gave me a lifelong aversion to cupcakes. There's no trace of a smirk on his lips like when told me his grandparents were nudists right before we pulled up to their house for a nice Sunday supper. Instead, I'm met with the same earnest stare as when he first told me that he loved me.

"Mack, what are you talking about? We have school on Monday. Why are you fucking with me?" His eyes don't change. He doesn't bust out laughing and revel in the "gotcha" moment.

"I know we do. I'm just going for a campus visit. Once you're admitted, you can go check out the school for a week and get a feel for it. I'm not going for good until July." He runs his hand over his dark brown hair and sweeps it down over his neck.

My mind is spinning out of control. I might black out. *Am I drunk? Is this a dream?*

"You're serious? You just decided to drop this on me? On prom night? How long have you been planning this? When did you even apply?" I'm being tossed around on a sea of anger and despair.

I'm drowning.

"I didn't want to just drop it on you. I applied last summer and I've been jumping through all their hoops for almost a year. It's a huge process. I had to get endorsed by our congressman. My athletic ability, my SAT scores, my leadership skills, like every little thing had to be proven and was analyzed. I didn't want to do all that, to try so hard and then have you and everyone else pity me if I didn't get it."

"This is crazy!" I jump to my feet and grab my clothes. "I can't believe you'd make a huge decision like this," I hop on one foot as I try to get my foot back into my twisted panties, "and not even mention it once." I step into my dress and tug it back up over my shoulders, "what about my scholarship here? You know I can't just walk away from that and go out east. Dammit, I haven't even applied to any schools in New York! Zip this up will ya?" I jerk my thumb over my shoulder and Mack complies. His fingers send little tingles down my spine, but I blink hard and bury the sensation letting my disbelief and confusion rule the show. "Didn't you think about me for one second? What kind of an asshole does this?"

If he wanted to make me yell, well he got his wish.

"Whoa, hold up. Of course I thought about you, but are you thinking about me? Christ, I thought you'd be proud of me. I thought you of all people would understand how important this is to me. You've known that I wanted to join the military ever since Ben …" his voice wavers.

I remember when his brother died. It's a day our entire nation remembers and mourns. We were fifteen and Mack was so proud of his big brother going out to New York City for a low level finance job after graduating college. We watched in horror as the twin towers were attacked. They tumbled down in slow motion, over and over, on every news station in the country.

Mack and his parents held onto hope that Ben had called in sick that day, or showed up late. However, as they left voicemail after voicemail that would never be returned, I watched the hope slowly deflate out of their bodies.

When we saw the groups of strangers and co-workers standing on window ledges, their hands forming a chain of solidarity as they jumped from the burning buildings, we cried. I held Mack in my arms as his body shook with sobs. He screamed at the television as he choked on his tears, "Why are you jumping? You can still get out! Why are they jumping?" He wanted so badly to believe that somehow they could still be rescued. Like there would be a back stairway that wasn't a burning column of smoke. Like there would be a ladder high enough to reach them.

It was the only time in my life that I've ever seen him cry.

Later, when it was finally confirmed that Ben had perished that day, Mack confided in me that he actually hoped his brother had been one of the jumpers. He liked the idea that he met God on his own terms, and didn't suffer.

I've known since that day that Mack wanted to join the military. Since the day he had lost Ben, the day our nation had its heart torn out, he'd sworn he'd fight the war on terror if given the chance. However, I'd always thought he would join a local unit and that we'd still have our life together here in Colorado. I had no idea that he would try to join the most elite military academy in the country. But then again, Mack never does anything small.

"Do you have any idea how hard it is to get into West Point? They only accept, like, ten percent of the people who apply you know," he continues. "You can't be over twenty-three, you can't be married, you can't have kids, you have to pass the interviews, the mental testing," he's ticking off each point on his fingers.

He's running out of fingers.

I shut my eyes for a second and take a deep breath. I feel like

I'm watching each milestone of our future together disappear with every admission criteria he rattles off.

"Community leader," Mack says.

Poof! There goes the vision of us as a cute elderly couple on a Sunday stroll.

"Medical testing," he continues.

Poof! Our wedding evaporates from the timeline.

"Fitness test," his voice is distant now.

Poof! The futon sex and ramen dinners shrivel up and blow away in a pile of dust.

"Are you even listening to me?" I open my eyes and Mack is standing in front of me. The inches between us feel like miles. For the first time, I realize he still hasn't gotten dressed, his hard muscles and thick cock are as exposed as his soul and I can't bear to look at any of it.

"Yes, I was just thinking. I *am* proud of you, Mack. I really am." My voice cracks. "But what about us? I thought we were forever, you and I." Fat tears gather in the corners of my eyes and I blink quickly.

"Lauren, we can still be together. There's lots of couples who do the long distance thing through college." He gently grasps my hand and for just a fleeting moment I believe him. I mean, sure, I've never heard of a long distance relationship working, like ever. Hey, I could be wrong. *Right?*

"And then what?" Reality creeps back in, cuffing me in the back of the head. "What about when we graduate? Won't you have to go on tour? Or get posted? It doesn't sound like this is only four years of distance, Mack. It sounds like a lifetime. I … I just can't do that."

"What are you saying? You want to break up?" His face twists up and his eyes squint like the revelation is blinding him. Surely he must have thought this was a possibility?

"No, I don't want to break up. I want you to stay here and go to Colorado U with me, like you made me think you were going to. I want you to grow old with me and I want to have your babies someday. You're the one running off to the east coast to make yourself feel better about a bad memory." I bite my tongue but the words had already slipped out. I can't take them back. Mack steps back like my stupid remark physically knocked into him.

"My brother," he seethes the words through his teeth, "isn't just some memory. And if you can't support me and my dream, if you can't be fucking happy for me that I earned something and fought hard for it, then this looks like it was the best decision of my life, cause it's saving me from waiting another ten years to find out what a waste of time this relationship has been."

My hand flashes in front of my face like a hummingbird wing, a sting spreads through my palm as it lands across his cheek. Luckily, the sound of the slap drowns out the sound of my heart breaking. We both stare at each other, tears blur my eyes and slide down my cheeks.

"I want to go home," my voice is ice. Mack doesn't grab me and pull me close, or run his hand through my hair and tell me it's all going to be ok. Instead, he slips his clothes back on and steps up into the golf cart, staring straight ahead, his jaw is set.

I slide in next to him and we sit in silence as we drive back toward the country club. The air has a chill to it now and as it whooshes around my ears, I can hear our love story again on the wind. But this time, it's being told in past tense.

And nothing will ever be the same again.

CHAPTER 5:

Year-2012

Mack

"*I*'ll be happy when we're done winning over hearts and minds for the day, sir." Corporal Thompson mutters as the camera crew is busy taking shots of the landscape for their footage. Landscape. That's hilarious. By landscape I mean endless sea of sand. We're not on high enough ground to really enjoy the mountains that Afghanistan has to offer, instead we're deep in her bowels. Gritty, dirty, brown expanses for as far as the eye can see.

"Keep your head up, Corporal. This last Shura will be about forty-five minutes and then we can get back to the base for some grub." I reassure him.

Truth is, I'm not so sure how much time we should be wasting on these Shura expeditions either. Every time we trek all over hell's half acre to meet the village elders and have a pow-wow with them about how we're here to help, not hurt, them and their kids, I can't help but feel like we're the butt of a national joke.

People aren't idiots, they know a propaganda campaign when they see one. It's difficult to occupy a country in war and also try to convince its citizens that you're not the enemy. That's the real battle, and I'm not sure we're ever gonna win that one.

"I'll tell ya, I can't wait to get back. I hope with the time difference it's not too late to get a hold of Nadine," Thompson squints and twists his head as he tries to solve the time zone equation in his head. "Three weeks. It's crazy how it's so short, but feels so long."

"It'll fly by, Corporal." I reassure him.

But I know it's a lie.

Kids waiting for Christmas ain't got nothing on us. After over 14 months of duty, the last three weeks will make molasses look like an Olympic sprinter. In some ways it feels like I was just getting settled into camp yesterday. In other ways it feels like this stretch of time has somehow expanded beyond my own lifeline. Like I was born into this war. Like I'll die from it.

"Don't worry, you'll be back with her soon."

I watch as the camera crew from CNB gathers around the silver haired news anchor who's come to capture a glimpse of our time over here. They've been following us for damn near a week, pulling guys aside with little interviews, and generally disrupting our routine. It's the nature of the beast though. Without news coverage, we'd get no support back home. People get too caught up in the morality of the war, and forget that there are *real* people torn from their *real* lives fighting it.

The news guy, Cooper Sanders, has been great as far as these guys go. He's been real gung-ho about experiencing everything for himself. When I first met him, I wrote him off as just another Hollywood type. Full of Botox and bravado, but he's kept up with us pretty good. Even running an obstacle course we threw together, in full gear, just for shits and giggles. He's good in my books. Even if he does wear make-up.

I let my eyes travel over to his personal make-up artist, Tiffany. She's clearly been watching me for a while cause her face lights up like a light bulb when she notices my gaze.

I shouldn't have fucked her.

"I hope you're right, Captain," Thompson continues. "I just got a bad feeling ya know? I know there's only a few weeks left, but I keep thinking this is when we're gonna get in the shit. If I could cut it short and go home today, I'd be on the first flight out. I just wanna be back with my woman and meet my son!"

"We know, Thompson. We know." Corporal Armstrong interrupts. "Most of the guys just wanna get home and get some poon, man. You though ... all you keep going on about is meeting a baby. Me, I'm gonna get back to the US and try to make babies with every girl who gives me the time of day. Just try to make em, mind ya. Not get all hormonal about actually having them, like this guy." Armstrong throws his arm around Corporal Thompson's neck and tugs his head under his armpit in a headlock.

"Screw off, Armstrong," he twists his head back out and takes a step back. "I'm not getting hormonal, I've got my first kid back home and I've never even met him. You don't get it. Until you can find someone who'll love you for more than a night, or for more than fifty bucks, you won't understand."

"Well, your mama don't mind all the fifty dollar bills I've been throwing her way. Just sayin'" Armstrong teases him.

"Man, my mama is a nice lady. I keep telling ya, she's a good, God loving woman. She wouldn't have nothing to do with your low-life ass." Thompson smiles. After more than a year together, the guys all chuck shit at each other and laugh it off pretty quickly. They say that the Marines is a brotherhood, but I'd say it's more than that. I'd always gotten along with my own brother, but the bond I have with these guys runs deeper than blood.

"What about you, Captain? You gonna get home and find yourself a good woman to settle down with? Or you gonna throw fifty bucks at Thompson's mama?" Armstrong asks with a twinkle in his eye. Thompson gives him a nudge in the ribs with his elbow but doesn't say anything to defend his poor mother, this time.

"Nah, you boys know I'm married to the Marines. She's been

keeping a roof over my head and feeding me three square meals a day since I was eighteen." I answer.

"From the doe-eyes that make-up chick's been watching you with, I'd say you already slayed some pussy over here, didn't ya?" Armstrong says too loudly.

He hasn't changed since the jock I knew in high school. When I first got off my leadership course and was assigned leadership of this platoon, I was shocked as shit to see him in my ranks. Cameron Armstrong was our school's big quarterback. He was supposed to head off to university and play college football for the Colorado Buffaloes.

Instead, he followed his gut to the military. I've asked him, off-side, if he regrets it. He said the only thing he'd ever change is that he would have joined the army sooner. That being said, Armstrong's contract is expiring soon after this tour and he's made it clear that he's still gonna go play college ball. We like to bust his balls and tell him the Buffaloes won't take on a geriatric like him, but he just brushes it off. Truth be told, if anyone has the swagger, skill and gumption to get out of the military and go back to school to play some football, it's Armstrong. I look forward to watching him play one day.

"Keep it down, Armstrong!" I hiss, popping my head up like a gopher to see if Tiffany heard. From the friendly smile on her face she didn't seem to. Or, if she did, she didn't care. Instead, she bats her fake eyelashes at me and gives me an exaggerated wink.

Don't dip your pen in the company ink, they say. Even though she's not military, she's here under our care. I should've known better than to fuck her brains out the first chance I got. And the second. And that third time was just greedy. Damn it, fourteen months is a long time with my old right hand, palm-ala. It's not like you can just go into town here and pick up chicks. That's a good way to get your dick blown off.

"I knew it, you dog." Armstrong's eye's light up. He's got me and he knows it. "Good for you, Captain. I would've got in there myself, but you must've been waiting at the ready for her, huh?"

"Something like that." I brush him off. The last thing I want to do is get into the nitty-gritty of how I fucked big tits Tiffany over there in the back of a U.S. military vehicle. I don't need rumors like that following me around.

"Whatever, you two have no idea what you're missing by chasing all that tail all the time. Someday, if you're lucky, you guys will find someone. I'm telling you, when you find a girl like my Nadine, it puts all this in perspective. I never thought anything would be more important to me than the army, but now I've got my son and my woman. It just changes man, you'll see. You'll meet someone who'll throw you off your game and make you forget all about this," Thompson sweeps his arm across the dusty landscape.

"Ha! Wanna put some money down on that one?" I shake my head; I can't even imagine a world where anything means more to me than the military. It's just the way I'm built. "Nah, you can have your domestic bliss, Thompson. I've got all I need with the army."

"Hey, Captain!" Cooper Sanders trots over to us, dust billowing around his feet as he takes each step. "We've got the shots we needed now. Thanks for being so patient with us." He smiles and his eyes crinkle into a spider web of fine lines. However, no other wrinkles form on his face. For a man with a full head of silver hair, his face is suspiciously free from aging.

"All right, form up!" I stand up straighter and call out to my platoon. Our group is forty strong, plus the CNB crew adding another eight. The men stop gaggling around and line up. They know that our break is over.

"We've got one more Shura to do, then we'll be calling it a day. I know it's been a long one. I know you're tired and hungry and your body just wants your bunk, but let's end this on a good note, boys!" I call out, and watch my guys straighten up and shake off the oppressive heat and dirt to focus on our next job. You can always count on a soldier to put the job first. I would trust each and every one of my boys with my life.

No question.

CHAPTER 6:

Year-2012

Mack

Cooper and his crew are up front with me as we put our boots to the ground and head down to the last stop of the day. The little village of Gumbad is only about fifteen minutes up the road. Fifteen minutes can feel like five hours when you've been out in the sand since dawn, but I know my platoon will suck it up and finish strong. Just like they always do.

"You know, Captain Forrester, I keep hearing about what your guys plan to do in three weeks. But I don't know what you're going to do when you get back to the United States." Behind Cooper, his camera man is recording us. There are no offline chats when you've got a news anchor shadowing you. Every thought, every movement, every facial expression is bound to be recorded, edited and used in their show.

The dust puffs around our boots and billows up to my knees. On dry days like this, I'm always reminded of pigpen from Charlie Brown. That kid must've done some time on the ground over here. Cause I'm pretty sure that when you get back from a deployment the dirt just hovers around you for life. Your own cloud of misery and filth, following you from the desert to your grave.

"When I get back? Well, after I soak all this dirt out of my pores, I'm planning on doing a cross-country tour on my bike." My heartbeat slows and my skin almost feels cool as I imagine the wind in my hair as I speed down the open freeway.

"Bike?" Cooper drags me back from my mental excursion to reality. "What kind of bike?" He watches me closely, too closely. His blue eyes analyzing my face almost as much as the unblinking eye of the camera.

"A Harley Davidson Fat Boy Lo." I answer simply. I blink, and for a split second, I imagine that the ruck sack digging into my back is the protective metal plates in my leather jacket. That the gritty path beneath my combat boots is the crunch of asphalt under my tires. I scan the barren road we're walking down and the glittering beige sandbox stretched out before me brings me back to the present.

"Harley? You want to end a fifteen-month tour by crossing the United States on your motorcycle?" Cooper tilts his head and his lips curl up into a half-cocked smile. I'm not sure if he's impressed or if he's laughing at me. Either way, I don't care.

"Yes, sir. I've been riding for over ten years now. I've taken a lot of small trips here and there, but I've never done a coast-to-coast ride. That's gonna change when I get back."

"Don't you want to spend some R & R on a beach or something? Maybe spend a few weeks at an all-inclusive resort? And, you know, relax a little?" He keeps pace with me without ever removing his piercing stare from my face. It's not like I've been going easy on him either, this whole week Cooper has been keeping up with us like a pro. The guy lugging the camera on his shoulder, capturing our "intimate chat" impresses me even more.

"No offense, sir. But, what kind of an idiot would I have to be to want to spend time on a sandy beach after spending over a year here? If I never see a beach again, I'll die happy I think."

Cooper laughs, a little pink creeps up into his cheeks as he shakes his head from side to side. "Yeah, I guess that wasn't the best example," he looks over his shoulder to his camera man sheepishly. He's only thrown off for a second though before he's back to his poker face, staring into my soul.

"Fair enough, I can understand why you wouldn't want to spend time on a beach then," he continues, "but what I mean is, don't you just want some time to relax? Don't you need a little time to decompress after all this?" Cooper is back on his game.

The wind suddenly picks up and whips some sand at my face. I squint and keep my head down, watching my boots navigate through the filthy fog of dust as I wait for it to pass. I remember when we first got over here and these dust ups would feel like razors against my cheeks, but now my skin is like a leatherback turtle. And my shell is just as hard to crack.

Once the swirling dirt settles back down, I scan the horizon. The village of Gumbad is in sight now. The little clay houses punctuating the vast expanse of nothingness. The day is almost done. One more X on the calendar. One day closer to home.

"Well, sir, I think relaxing and decompressing look different to everyone. Most of my guys are gonna go home after this and spend time with their loved ones, or binge watch the tv shows they've missed over the past year, and that's what they need to do. It's what they *deserve* to do after all this."

As we keep trudging forward I can see a handful of young boys kicking a soccer ball in bare feet. One of the boys points to my platoon and picks the ball up, tucking it under his arm. His friends stop and watch as we approach, cupping their hands over their eyes like makeshift sunglasses.

"To me, there's nothing more peaceful than when I watch the sunset as I drive over the horizon on my bike. The calm that washes over me, well, no amount of Netflix can give me that. It's just who I am, I guess." I shrug.

Cooper looks satisfied with himself. Maybe I gave him some

good footage, I don't know. His focus turns to the village a few yards away and his camera man adjusts his shot accordingly.

The boys suddenly run back toward the houses and elderly village men shuffle out to greet us in their place.

"Willoby! Move up!" I yell over my shoulder. "Company, halt!" The forty pairs of boots crack to a stop like a clap of thunder. Willoby is by my side, ready to translate for me as I disengage from the platoon to make introductions.

Stepping forward, with my arm extended, I try to look friendly and relax my face as my eyes scan the village behind them. A large group of children are running around, excited by our presence. The ladies are huddled together by a wash basin, whispering to each other and eyeing us suspiciously.

I shake the hand of the man in front, noting his long white beard and deep wrinkles before my eyes settle on his. Willoby introduces me and the elder welcomes us to Gumbad. It's the same routine we've been doing all day. It's the same for every Shura. Right out of the manual and PowerPoint presentations we're given. Just like everything in the military, there's protocol to follow.

I give the command to move my company forward and we make our way closer to the huts. The children run around my men like they're trying to herd them together, circling them excitedly. After posting four men as lookouts, we sit together on the ground. We take off our helmets, laying them in front of our crossed legs, and lay our rifles down as a show of good faith. Again, protocol.

Regulations. Orders. There's a disciplined and planned way to do everything in the army.

Cooper sits in the dirt next to me, he stays quiet as Willoby chats with the elders. His camera crew focus on the talk, I can't imagine they'll use much of this footage. It can't be very interesting tv to watch a translator and old man make small talk in another language.

My eyes wander over to the women and children standing off to our left. The women whisper to each other, looking over at us nervously. This isn't new. Having a group of armed men around them and their kids would be enough to make any mother anxious.

"Can you ask him how old he is? And how many wars he's lived through?" Cooper asks my translator.

As he asks the questions, I notice the women begin to gather the children into a group as they move them away from us. My head snaps as I quickly look around us. Suddenly, the village is deserted except for the men sitting with us. Checking back on the group of women, they have picked up the pace, scurrying now to put distance between them and us.

The boy who held the soccer ball under his arm as we approached looks back at us as one of the women yanks his arm. My gut twists and the blood rushes in my ears as I jump to my feet. "Troops! Grab your weapons!"

The words barely escape my lips when one of the village men jumps up, pulling an ax from under his robe and runs at Corporal Thompson. I snatch up my gun and hastily snap on my helmet as I watch the man raise his arm and split Thompson's head open with a thud. The sound of the ax sinking into my young Corporal's brain sounds too faint to be real. Too far off, and too quiet to account for all the blood pouring out of the young Corporal and into the dirt.

"Shit!" I pull my gun into my shoulder and squeeze the trigger, dropping the man.

BOOM! Dirt explodes into a mushroom cloud around us. *Fuck! Did someone set off a bomb? Was that an IED? Christ.* I can barely make out the silhouettes of my men scrambling to position. Shots are being fired in the dusty haze.

My eyes finally adjust to the filth falling from the sky and focus on Cooper Sanders. He's just standing, staring into the chaos as gunfire explodes around him. *Damn it! He's not even wearing his fucking helmet! What the hell is he doing?* Suddenly a green egg drops to his feet, he doesn't move, he's still just staring. Like he's waiting for a little birdie to pop out instead of being frozen to the spot as a grenade is about to blast at his feet.

I look over to his right, and Armstrong is lying on his belly, desperately fighting to fix a jam on his rifle. A jam means no bullets. No bullets mean death.

I've got to do something! I run to Cooper, throwing him to the side and kick the grenade like it's the soccer ball we saw the boys playing with earlier. As the edge of my boot catches the casing, I can feel it fly away. Then a blast of hot air surrounds my leg as the grenade explodes. I'm lifted through the air like a pillow being tossed around at a teen girl's slumber party before my back thuds into the dirt and I roll another ten feet. My ears squeal the horrific siren song of war; my eardrums must be fucked.

I manage to push myself up onto my elbows and look at the scene unfolding in front of me like some kind of Scorsese wet dream. Blood and fragments of skin and bone are painting the beige ground a deep maroon as my men continue to fight off the ambush. My leg feels like someone is pouring hot water down it, when I look down my eyes confirm what my mind and body already knew: *it's gone.*

There's no time for that right now! Another explosion sends dirt flying everywhere and I flip over onto my stomach and use my good leg and my elbows to drag me back over to Cooper. He hasn't moved from where I threw him, I'm not sure if he's dead, but I know he's unarmed. The sand grates against my exposed skin and the feeling of hot water running over my leg continues. Somehow, I crawl to Cooper. He's not dead. Maybe injured. Definitely in shock. But not dead.

"Fuck! What the hell is happening!" he screams. *I guess I can hear after all; the blast must've just phased me.* I lay over him like a sandbag and raise my rifle. Pop! Pop! Pop! I squeeze the trigger, aiming for the center of mass, or the heart as civilians say. Another man from the village drops to the dirt.

I can hear the whirling rotor blades of a Blackhawk overhead. *Thank you, Jesus.* Keeping Cooper still beneath me, I raise my rifle, scanning for another fighter to come into view. However, I don't see any through the heavy fog of sand.

"Captain! Captain! We've got to take you out!" I twist my head over my shoulder to see 3 medics with a stretcher running up behind me.

"I'm not going anywhere without my men!"

"Captain, you're bleeding out. If we don't get you out of here you're gonna die," the young medic yells in my ear as he pulls my shoulders. I feel several hands on me as I'm lifted from Cooper. Lifted from the ground and put on the stretcher.

"How many did we lose? Did we get them all?" I yell.

"Don't worry about that right now, you'll be debriefed later. Right now we need to get you back to the base."

I wince as they strap me to the board. Looking down over my body, I see my skin hanging from just below my knee in long flaps. Blood spreads over the stretcher in the place where my limb should be. My leg is gone. *It's gone.* For the first time, my mind has a chance to process the thought.

I'm carried to the Blackhawk and maneuvered inside. I close my eyes as one of the medics begins tying off a tourniquet to slow the bleeding.

Gone.

I don't know how many of my men are dead, but I know I've lost some. My men are gone. My friends. My brothers. Dead.

As the wraps are tied down tight around my leg, I can feel us lifting up in the Helo. I used to love helicopter rides. The thrill of soaring through the air, usually to be dropped somewhere exciting and new. I close my eyes and try to slow my breathing. I need to calm down.

I need to ….

Lauren!

Her soft brown eyes and glowing almond skin race through my mind. I can smell fresh lilacs, her perfume. I can taste her gloss on my lips. I swear, I can feel her holding my hand as I'm lifted to the medical center.

I need her.

CHAPTER 7:

Year-2014

Mack

"So where did you disappear to, Captain America?" Corporal Lopez twists around in his passenger seat to shoot a knowing smile my way. "Can you believe this guy?" He jerks his thumb at me in the backseat as his attention falls on our driver, Specialist Parsons. "He's got a whole pussy parade after him all night, rubbing up on him like cats in heat, and then he just plucks the two prettiest ones from the bunch and takes off."

In the rear view mirror I can see Parsons lift his eyebrows skyward. His moustache raises up higher when he does it, giving his face the appearance of a human arrow.

"Oh yeah? Two of 'em, huh?"

I don't respond, but the night before flashes in my mind. I can see their crimson lips brushing against each other as they slid their tongues from the base of my cock all the way up to the tip at the same time. My dick twitches up against my zipper, as if it's reminding me that he had a great time when both the blonde and brunette from the night before slid their tongues up and around me like strippers on a pole.

"It was a good night," I admit to my reflection in the window as I watch the familiar Colorado scenery float by me. I haven't been back here since I left for West Point about a decade ago. I'm struck by the little things that've changed almost as much as I am by all the things that never did.

"A good night," Lopez snorts over his shoulder at me, rolling his eyes. "You should've seen this greedy bastard in there, those girls were grinding up on him like a Roman orgy every time he got a drink at the bar. Man, that Captain America name is gold too. Did you come up with that or what?"

I didn't.

It was just insanely good timing that the news footage of the firefight in Afghanistan hit the media outlets at the same time as the blockbuster movie hit the screens. Once Cooper Sanders got back on the air, he did a segment about the "real Captain America" who saved his life. Well, that was that. Fox, CNB and everyone else picked it up and ran with it.

I don't love it, being compared to a comic book character makes me feel uneasy about the men I lost. Like watching Thompson get his head split open like a walnut is the same as watching a scene in a movie theatre. Like my men who didn't make it are just extras on a set. Like the flashbacks and nightmares are exciting little trailers teasing this summer's big Hollywood hit.

Captain America feels like it's downplaying what happened over there for the sake of a quippy nickname. It feels like we're trading compassion for sound bytes. But, I can't change it, and it makes the girls practically cum as soon as they lay eyes on me. Not that bringing ladies home was ever a problem before. But, Lopez is right, now it's as easy as pointing at one, two, hell, even three of them and heading out.

"Nah, I picked it up from one of those news shows. Who gives themselves a nickname anyway?" I shake my head.

"Yeah, Parsons, who would do something like that? That would just be *weird*, wouldn't it Captain Forrester?" Lopez twists in his seat again to face our driver, who looks a little red in the face.

"Shut up, man." Parsons tenses his jaw and his shoulders stiffen. I can't help but laugh.

"Seriously? I gotta hear this one. What was the name?" I watch Parsons silently plead with Lopez in a single look. For a second, I think the Corporal is gonna stop chucking shit at his friend and leave me in the dark. Then he turns around in his seat, his eyes are twinkling like a cat that caught a little bird to snack on.

"Yeah, man, what was it you wanted everyone to call ya?" He pushes Parsons, but the only response is a flood of red rising up the back of my driver's neck as he stares straight forward, unblinking.

"The sperminator," Lopez looks me straight in the face and answers. Parsons turns a shade of purple usually reserved for eggplants and stroke victims.

"You're a dick, man." He manages to push the words through his locked jaw.

Lopez starts laughing like a hyena and I can't help but laugh too.

"What? Why would you even *want* that to catch on?" Tiny tears form in the corners of my eyes as I struggle to breathe through my laughter.

"I dunno, I thought chicks would think it sounded cool. Fuck I was seventeen, you think you can drop it?" Parsons snaps at us but Lopez and I keep laughing.

"Dicks."

The scenery blurs by the car window like fragments of a dream. At least it's not like my real dreams. Instead of the sand covered hellhole full of bodies that I visit every night, I see the field I used to play little league on. Instead of the village that I keep walking into in my sleep, I see my old middle school.

Memories piece together and remind me of my roots. I haven't been back since I left for West Point, I was on my first tour when my parents packed up and headed to the sunshine state for retirement, so I never had reason to come home. A decade has gone by and I try to distract myself with all the little things that have changed. That strip mall never used to be there. Those subdivisions are new. It's all a nice distraction from the only thing left in Colorado I care about.

Lauren.

Giving my head a shake, I push the thought away. If I've learned anything over the years, it's that there's no shortage of pussy. After all, I got my leg blown off, not my dick. Although, there's been many women who've tried to suck it off. Who am I to deny them?

After almost a year of intensive treatment at Walter Reed, the military gave me a choice: I could continue to be active duty or head out onto civvie street. It seemed like a no-brainer. I live to serve. Then I found out "active duty" meant desk jockey. Nope. No way I'm gonna stamp piles of paperwork for eight hours a day for the next fifteen years. Nothing against those guys, but I need something with a bit more adrenaline pumping through it's veins. Something a bit more dangerous than maybe getting a paper cut.

When they told me I could discharge and finish my treatment at the Spalding Center near my hometown, I agreed. I mean, what else was I gonna do? Go hang out in an orange grove with my parents in Florida? Besides the military, Colorado has been the only home I've ever known.

I stare out my window blankly at the city sliding by. Suddenly, my eyes snap to focus when I see the red, white and blue flapping crisply in the spring wind. A row of flags lines the street, out the other window it's the same. The blue on the flags compete with the blue of the sky. Parsons turns the corner and the road is lined down both sides with motorbikes, firemen, police and a ton of folks cheering.

A bunch of them are holding signs. "Welcome home." "American Hero!" I wasn't expecting this. The car slows down, and we pass hundreds of people waving and smiling. I roll down the window and wave back. On the sidewalk I see a pretty young thing with a couple of kids standing knee high to her. One of the boys stands straight and brings his little hand to his temple in a salute. I'm no softie, but I feel my heart twinge as I raise my hand to salute back at him.

The crowd seems endless; hell I've seen Veteran's Day parades with less turn out. I know that when the footage first got released of me kicking the grenade away from Cooper, I was getting all kinds of attention. Interviews with 20/20, 60 minutes, even Oprah sat down with me. As the months in recovery wore on, the media buzz died down.

Unfortunately, so did all the fan mail from women who were offering me marriages and a womb to put my kids in. The wedding offers didn't do anything for me, but some of the nasty descriptions of what they wanted to do to me to show their gratitude helped me get through some dark times. Luckily, when I was allowed to leave the hospital and mingle in the community, many more women were all too happy to show me just how grateful they really were. And flexible. If there's anything better than a hot piece of ass with a patriotic streak and a deep throat, I don't want to know.

No, wait, I do want to know. Send her my way.

"Well, holy shit Captain, it looks like the whole state came out to see you," Lopez mutters in awe.

He's not wrong, the street leading to the hospital is throbbing with people waving, shaking signs welcoming me over their heads and people giving me a thumbs up or salute.

A thunderous roar behind us makes me jump in my seat and twist around, fraying my nerves. For a second, my mind flashes to the desert and I expect to see a formation of Humvees rattling through the dust. Instead, I see a motorcycle group is roaring their engines as they follow the car in a different sort of convoy. My heart stops beating wildly in my chest and instead, I feel myself fighting to keep a lump in my throat from forming as I watch the group trail us in a v-formation, like a pack of Canadian geese heading south for the winter, with our car leading the way.

"I feel like I'm driving the president or something," Parsons finally speaks again. I guess the crowd is even impressive enough to make him forget about the whole sperminator thing. For now, anyway.

He slows to a crawl as we make our way past the smiling faces. I could get out and walk faster than we're driving and I've got one leg. It's not like he has much choice though, with all the kids jumping around the car and trying to run up beside us, we've got to be careful.

Finally, we pull up to the rehab center and I catch my first glimpse of the media scrum waiting for us outside the front doors.

The parking lot is overflowing with vehicles punctuated by full-sized, windowless vans with local and national news slogans and anchors faces plastered to the sides.

"Talk about a hero's welcome," Lopez smiles back at me, but the corners of his mouth quickly settle down into a straight line when he sees my face. "Hey, are you ok, Captain? You look a little distant." His eyes dart over my face as I swallow my emotions and give myself a shake.

"Yeah, I'm fine. I just wasn't expecting all this," I answer truthfully. I won't bother him with the detail about how just a noise brought me back to a war I left almost a year ago. He doesn't need to know that simple sounds have the ability to make me jump outta my skin. No one needs to know that.

"Whaddya expect," Parsons interrupts, "he's probably overwhelmed with how much pussy he's gonna get here, right Forrester?" His eyes twinkle at me in the rear view mirror and I give out a laugh too loud for the joke.

"Yeah man, you know it. Just scoping out my first hits back here," I nod and Lopez watches me a bit too closely then nods back, and turns back around in his seat.

"Alright, we're here," Parsons announces as he pulls the car up to the curb of the hospital. I can see that the staff have had the foresight to cordon off the crowd from the entrance so I'll be able to make it inside without being mobbed. Or maybe they did it so the media would be able to get better shots of my arrival. Camera crews line both sides of the sidewalk leading to the front doors of the building, waiting for my big entrance. As Parsons jerks the car to a stop and the guys jump out to retrieve my wheelchair from the trunk, I curse the stupid procedure that requires me to wheel into the building rather than walk in like I've been practicing now for seven months.

Once I've lowered myself into the chair, I can feel Lopez try to grab the bars behind me to push me toward the building, but I grab the wheels with both hands and jerk them forcefully under my control, making it clear I don't need his help. He lets go and the two men flank my sides as we make our way up the sidewalk together.

"We love you, Captain America!" I hear some women cry out and I scan the crowd to see if they're worth acknowledging. My eyes settle on a small group of young, tight, blondes bouncing up and down with a glittery sign over their head. The sign itself gives me a moment's pause as I notice that they've cut out a picture of the movie character, Captain America, in his blue tights and everything and they've pasted my face over his. Seeing yourself in a patriotic, skin-tight bodysuit is jarring, but I get over it pretty quickly as I watch them jiggle their perky tits in their tiny t-shirts. I imagine the four of them taking turns bouncing up and down on my cock like that, and all is forgiven about them making me look like a red, white and blue ballerina on their sign.

I push my chair up the path and soak in the scene as cameras flash non-stop. Even though it's bright outside, the small explosions of light are distracting. Memories of explosives flashing as they flung fragments of deadly metal at us wash over me. The grip on my wheelchair tires tighten and I breathe deep as I try to ground myself. Before I have a chance to get my mind back under control, I see a man hop over the metal barrier holding back the crowd and jog toward me with his hand inside his coat pocket.

"Shit." In an instant the crowd evaporates and the village is behind me. My skin prickles with sweat and I can see the man pulling an axe out from under his billowy robes seconds before I know it's about to plunge into Thompson's skull. I jump from my seat, fist clenched and grab the man roughly by the arm.

Lopez jumps between us and I lose my grip as he puts distance between our bodies. I blink as the village disappears and the man's clothes transform back into a windbreaker and jeans before my eyes.

The crowd shrieks and claps like a rock star just jumped on a stage when they see me jump to my feet. Our little situation on the sidewalk is blanketed with the sound of whoops and hundreds of clapping hands.

The man looks at Lopez and pulls a pad of paper out of his pocket and nods at me, "Hey man, I just want an autograph. Can you sign it for me?"

I look down at the folded up paper of Captain America's face smiling up at me and cameras flash like strobe lights around us. My head spins and my stomach feels like liquid, but I manage to push it down and I think I'm even smiling. Hopefully it looks like a smile and not a snarl as I grab the paper and sign my name. The crowd seems satisfied with it as they erupt into another round of cheers. I stand taller and scan the unfamiliar faces. How many people came out to wish me well today? It's incredible that so many people I've never met care about me so much.

My eyes fall over old and young faces, none of them familiar, yet all of them friends. Wait, is that Lauren? I squint at the back of the crowd, closest to the door of the facility. Did she come out to see me come back after all these years? Her brown skin glows warmly and I can almost see the emotions in her eyes. Is she happy to see me? Or disappointed?

"Sir?" A small hand tugs on my sleeve, stealing my attention. I look down into the face of a little girl, her round cheeks covered in freckles and her broad, gap-toothed smile. "Sir?" she repeats.

"Yes?"

"Can I take a selfie with you?" She blinks up at me and I can't help but smile.

"Sure kid. What's your name?"

"Bethany," she beams at me and holds a cellphone up to me. The crowd is starting to have more brave souls cross the barrier ever since the first guy jumped over. I don't have time to take pictures and sign a hundred sheets of paper. But, I'll make time for this kid. I quickly hold the phone up and we both smile up at the screen as I click our picture. Bethany squeezes my hand excitedly as I hand her back the cell.

"Thank you, sir. I can't believe I got a picture with you. Thank you!" She smiles and reminds me of candle lit jack-o-lanterns on doorsteps in October.

"No problem," I smile back before looking back up into the sea of people for the one person I recognized.

I search through the faces, eagerly looking for her, but Lauren is no where to be found. I must need more sleep than I thought. These late nights are catching up to me.

Whatever, give your head a shake. You're not here for her. Besides, with the look Lopez is giving me, I know I've got bigger fish to fry than wondering about some old girlfriend.

Now if I could just get my eyes to stop searching for her in the crowd and my heart to stop beating her name.

But, yeah, besides that. Totally over it.

CHAPTER 8:

Year–2014

Lauren

Why am I standing here? I told myself I was gonna wait this out in the staff room until someone dragged me out from my feeble attempt to hide behind the curtains or something. Instead, I'm out here with all the other "Captain America" groupies and fans.

Like Mack is just some guy I know from watching news footage of him kicking a grenade across the sand. Like I'm just another cheap girl in a crowd of cheap girls, trying to be noticed. Like we don't have real history. Like we don't have real love.

Didn't have, I mean. Of course we don't still have love. When he left me for West Point ten years ago, I was left wondering if we ever did.

I look over at the ladies in the hoard of people and instantly regret my stupid decision to not wear make-up today. I wanted to look professional, not like I was trying to get a date. Next to these girls I look like a corpse with my dull skin and my hair in a simple bun. I smooth my hands over my uniform and fold my arms around my body as I watch Mack push his chair toward the front doors.

Suddenly some idiot jumps over the barricade and moves toward Mack. When he stands up to greet the guy, everyone around me erupts into fervent cheering. Like he's some kinda rock star.

More like a cock star. If the stuff I found out on the internet about him is even half true, he's gonna sleep his way through the women in this crowd two or three at a time. Not that I'm stalking him or anything. Just checking up, that's all. Besides, from the look of these women, I don't think they'll mind being Mack's toy for a night. There's so much cleavage being thrust toward him; I'm surprised they aren't begging him to sign their boobs with a sharpie by now.

It's not like I care, but it's just kinda skanky if you ask me.

Now that Mack's standing, I can see his tattoos smothering every inch of his arms. There's some sort of flowers etched across his neck, peeping out from under his tight shirt. Not exactly the young man who left Colorado after grad.

EDDIE CLEVELAND

Only Mack Forrester could lose his leg and still swagger back into my life and make my heart stop.

Tattoos or not, I remember what every inch of that hard body looks like naked. My pulse pounds in my ears and heat rises in me like mercury in a thermometer. I don't mean to let my eyes drift over his cut biceps and down over the pronounced ripples in his shirt announcing his glorious abs to the world. It's not like I want to notice the curve of his tight ass and the bulge of his ....

I snap my eyes back up to his face and he's staring right into my eyes.

I. Can. Not. Breathe.

The air hisses from my lungs as I'm caught in the hypnotic trance of his blue eyes. So, I guess not that much has changed after all. The old feeling of butterflies erupts inside my chest, and even though their wings must be coated in dust after lying dormant for so long, they feverishly flurry around my heart.

I'm sure it's only a second. Hell, it's probably less than that, but I swear I can see an eternity in his crystal blue eyes. The moment of recognition that turned to lust and then, something deeper and truer than that. It's like the roadmap of our past being playing out in a single glance. When he finally looks away and I remember to actually fill my lungs again, I realize there's a part of me that hopes it's the roadmap to our future as well.

Part of me, *all* of me. Who's keeping track, right?

A firm hand on my shoulder nearly makes me jump out of my skin. I stifle a yelp as I wheel around to face Shannon. Somehow I manage to keep my eyes from rolling. Somehow I keep my mouth from tugging down at the corners. It's not that Shannon is the most annoying or the most incompetent nurse I've ever dealt with.

Oh wait, no, that's exactly it.

"Sorry to interrupt, Lauren," her face denies that she's feeling anything at all. Sympathy or otherwise. "I need you for a second inside." Her flat, robotic voice has a way of cutting through the noise around me and sucking the jubilation out of the moment.

Shannon. With her flat, bobbed hair plastered against the side of her head and her large, sad eyes she always makes me think of what Eeyore would look like in a nurse costume.

"Can it wait?" I manage to smile and can almost feel my fake happiness being sucked into the black hole that is her personality. "I have to give the tour in ten minutes." I jerk my thumb over my shoulder to the scene behind me and she looks up like she's just noticed the hundreds of people and cameras for the first time.

"No, sorry. I need you to sign off on Mr. Brookfield's discharge papers or he won't be able to leave in time to get to the airport. His wife is getting all upset. It'll probably take less than ten minutes though." She throws a bone of hope at me, but I know it's a lie. Nothing in nursing takes ten minutes. However, there's not much I can do. I knew I had to get that paperwork finished up this morning, I guess I just got distracted.

I glance over my shoulder one last time at my distraction. I'm normally diligent about crossing my t's and dotting my i's, but I think given the circumstances that forgetting Mr. Brookfield's papers is understandable. A group of young women start screaming like teen groupies, as if to confirm my story.

I look back into Shannon's dead eyes and sigh. "Ok, let's go."

CHAPTER 9:

Year - 2014

Mack

"**A**nd if you look out, across the field there, you'll see our outdoor track. Now that spring is here, I'm sure you'll put it to good use with your program." Dr. Galt smiles quickly at me and then holds his smile painfully for the cameras flashing around us. "But, since it is Colorado, you always have the option of the indoor track if we happen to get a freak snow storm in June or something," he chuckles at his own joke, the same joke he told when he gave us a tour of the inside track about twenty minutes ago.

I smile politely and try to pay attention, but damn it these nurses aren't making it easy for me. I can see that as the chief of medicine here, Dr. Galt is very proud of his facility. And he should be. It's top notch. From the indoor, Olympic sized pool and the state of the art physio equipment, he has every reason to wanna show it all off. There isn't a surface that isn't gleaming or a face that isn't smiling. It's just that my eyes are having a tough time paying attention to the shiny surfaces when there's just so many sultry smiles to focus on.

Every time I wheel through one of these stations, there's another piece of ass in a nurse's uniform giving me a wink as she runs her tongue over her lips, giving me ideas about what else she can do with that tongue and where else she can wrap those lips.

With all the media here, it's no surprise that all the ladies are looking their best. With their hair perfectly styled and enough make-up on that they look like they might be strippers dressed as nurses instead of medical professionals.

However, I know that it's really for me.

As if to confirm it, whenever a camera is rolling around them, the ladies are textbook class and professionalism. And as soon as the media strolls on by, the tits pop up and they start looking at me like the hungry kittens they are. Not that I mind. I've just gotta make sure I'm a bit more discerning with the ones I fuck at this place.

After almost a year in rehab at the military facility in Maryland, I had nurses practically clawing each other's eyes out when I spread myself too thin. This time I've gotta try to avoid the drama and be a bit choosier. Besides, I'm only supposed to be living here for a couple weeks and then I'll be doing the outpatient program during the day and going to my own place at night. That should make it a little easier to keep the ladies warming me up under the sheets under wraps.

Parsons looks like he's enthralled by the tour, ignoring all the easy pussy around us and hanging on the good doctor's every word. I'm surprised he doesn't have a little notepad out for jotting down the highlights from how interested he appears. Lopez, on the other hand, is scouting out the pickings, giving me raised eyebrows and tiny nods each time we turn a new corner and come across more tits and ass.

"If you'll follow me, down to the left," Dr. Galt interrupts the unspoken conversation between Lopez and I, directing us down another hall, "over here is where you'll find your room."

Finally! My attention fully snaps back into focus as I wheel behind Galt to see my new quarters. A sparkling rehab center is all well and good, but if they've got you stuffed in a broom closet with a bed, then none of it matters. Not that I'll have a problem breaking in the bed, even if it is in a broom closet.

My fears are quickly quelled when I follow the Dr. into the sprawling room. The bed looks comically small in the expansive space. With a leather couch against the wall and a huge tv mounted across from it, it's clear that this room isn't in a military facility. With the view of rolling hills out the window and the massive bathroom with a soaker tub and a walk in shower, I feel like this could be a suite at the Hilton, not a room in a hospital.

The camera crews and news anchors easily fit inside the space, carefully capturing my expression and the details of the décor for the five o'clock highlights.

A sweet little brunette in a pencil skirt and heels clicks her way across my room and sways her hips on over to my window. She acts like she's interested in the view, but I can see from how she's popping her heart shaped ass that she wants to make sure I'm the one soaking in the sights. Give the lady what she wants, that's what I say. I'm here to please.

"Captain, do you mind if Phil gets some footage of you checking out your room? I think the viewers will really be happy to see you looking settled in." She turns around from the window and smiles warmly. Her camera guy shuffles across the room and points the unblinking lens in my face, waiting for me to "act natural".

I push myself up from my chair and strut across the floor, closing the distance between her and I. Her heartbeat is visible in her collarbone as I brush past her and quickly look out over the mountains and lush grass outside. I can hear her breathe in sharply when I turn on my heel and saunter over to my bed, sitting on the edge carefully.

"Looks … comfy," the brunette locks her eyes on me and I can't help but smile at her flushed cheeks.

"It is."

Dr. Galt clears his throat loudly and the news anchor jumps like a kid trying to sneak back into their parents' house in the middle of the night. I don't bother turning around to face him as he tries to direct the crowd out of the room. Why would I look at a middle-aged, balding man when I can rest my eyes on full set of tits and hips?

"If all the members of the media would follow me, I'll take you to the conference room where I can answer any questions you may have about our facility," he urges.

The brunette looks at me and then over at the doctor, like she's not sure if she really has to go or not. However, she snaps out of her spell and makes her way back out the door with the rest of them.

"It's about time you showed up," I hear Galt scolding someone quietly. "Captain Forrester, I apologize, I know you're probably ready to settle in after a long day, but I'd like to introduce you to the nurse overseeing your program here. This is Nurse Brickman, and she'll be responsible for your care while you're with us."

I stand back up from the edge of my bed and instantly freeze on the spot.

The room is empty now, except for my military entourage and the remaining medical staff. There's no more flashing cameras or stripper nurses distracting me.

Yet, I still feel like I'm in some kind of dream, because standing in the doorway is a perfect vision from my past. Fixing me to the spot with her mahogany eyes is the most beautiful woman I've ever seen or ever will see.

My voice catches in my throat as I soak in the way the light radiates from each angle of her face. Highlighting her cheeks, making her kissable lips glisten perfectly. I want to run across the room and pick her up. I want to kiss her, to wrap my arms around her and never let her leave my side again. I want to throw her down on this bed and fuck her until we both forget our names and the time that's passed between us.

Instead, I'm stuck to the floor, staring. Somehow I manage to open my mouth. Somehow words tumble out.

"Hi, Lauren."

CHAPTER 10:

Year - 2014

Lauren

"Hi, Mack."

Is there an oxygen tank in this room? I might need someone to grab me a mask. On second thought, isn't there a defibrillator in the hall? I should get Dr. Galt to go grab that for me.

Speaking of the boss, he gives me a scowl for showing up late. His gaze softens like butter when he looks over my shoulder out into the hallway where the journalists are congregating. I can tell from the way he's looking at them longingly that he's not going to waste his time giving me a lecture right now.

Even though the crowd outside and all the news anchors showed up today for Mack, it's easy to see that Dr. Galt has been soaking this up like it's his moment. Wait a minute, I squint at his normally pale face, why does he look darker? The chief can usually drop planes out of the sky with his blindingly white skin, yet now he looks like he's actually gotten some sun. I see the telltale line of orangey-beige badly blended into his thinning hairline and realize he's either gone out and gotten a spray tan for his big moment under the spotlight, or he's wearing make-up.

I prefer to believe it's a spray-tan. Even if his hands are still practically translucent.

"Do you two know each other?" He flickers his eyes over my face quickly and then darts them back over my shoulder to the crowd waiting for him in the hall.

Mack opens his mouth and I stitch it shut with a single look. *Nope.* This isn't time for confessions.

"Yeah, we went to high school together." I quickly answer, heading off whatever is percolating in Mack's brain.

"Oh, good. Good. Ok. Well, uh, Nurse Brickman will go over your schedule with you. If you have any issues or questions, you can get a hold of me any time." He spits out the words quickly, as he watches the reporters like a kid who's desperate for his parents' attention.

"Ok, thank you. I appreciate the tour, Dr. Galt." Mack walks across the room and shakes his hand. My boss can barely find the enthusiasm to move his arm up and down a couple times before he abandons the handshake for the closest thing he's ever had to fans outside the door.

Mack's military escorts shake his hand and clap him on the shoulder before leaving us alone together.

Suddenly the biggest room in the hospital feels like it's folding in on itself as the space between us seems to disappear.

Space, time, distance. It's funny how your heart can so quickly forget the very things that ripped it in half.

I'm not sure if I want to kiss him or slap him, maybe both. Either way, I want an excuse to touch him.

"What?" I ask. I know that cocky smirk, like he just heard a punchline that he hasn't bothered to share yet.

"Brickman? Seriously?" He covers his smile with the palm of his hand and I realize slapping him would definitely be the better option.

"Yes, Brickman."

"You got married?"

"I did."

"To Joel Brickman?"

"That's the one."

"Do you have kids?"

"One."

"You got married and had kids with Joel fucking Brickman? Come *on*! I mean, I know when I left town there was slim pickings, but your science partner?" He rolls his eyes.

"At least Joel was there for me. Unlike some people." I snap at him. "Besides, you shouldn't speak badly about the dead." I rub the empty spot on my ring finger, regretting my decision to put my ring in a safety deposit box a couple of months ago. I told myself that it was time to stop wearing it when the anniversary of his death snuck up on me.

"He died?"

"Yeah, that's what that means." My words are tinged with frost.

The twinkle extinguishes from Mack's blue eyes and his smirk settles out into a line. "How? I mean, I'm sorry to hear that. He was so young!" I can see him trying to connect the dots.

"Yeah, he was hit in a head on collision. It was instant." My voice is flat and quiet, yet the words feel too loud.

"I'm sorry." Mack steps toward me and I hate to admit how much I want to throw my arms around his neck and nuzzle my head into his chest. How much I want to feel him run his thumb over the back of my head and to hear his voice tell me that it's all over now. That all the hardship, the heartache, the confusion, they're all in the past and that he's here to take away all my pain.

Instead, I step aside and walk over to the window, putting the space between us that I need in order to get my head on straight.

"I've been following your story. You know, like on the news and everything," I confess to the glass, taking a deep breath. I turn around and let myself get lost in his eyes once more. "I'm sorry about the men you lost, Mack. And about what you've been through."

His eyes flicker and for a moment he goes somewhere else. Somewhere far from Colorado. From me.

He shakes his head slowly and his eyes focus as he clears his throat. "Thanks. I'm just happy to be home now."

"I'm happy you're home too," my voice cracks. Damn it. "I, uh, I've got a great program outlined for you here," I stuff my hand in my pocket and pull out my phone so I can bring up his schedule. "I know you've been working hard on walking again, and I can see you've put in the hours with how well you're doing."

My mind snaps into nurse mode and I force my emotions back down my throat and bury them deep in my gut. "But, I'm gonna get you running again. By the time you're finished here, you'll be living the same as you did before the ..." I don't want to call it an accident. I saw the footage, just like the rest of America, and it wasn't some kind of tumble that took Mack's leg.

"Before I mistook a grenade for a soccer ball? I always get them confused. It's all those little octagon shapes on them. Practically identical." he jokes and I smile back at him, happy to let the awkward moment go.

I look down at the screen of my phone and see that my son's school has been calling and texting me.

What the? I scroll through the messages, piecing together the situation. Perfect. Just perfect.

"Everything ok, Lauren?" Mack hovers near me and I can smell his scent. The little hairs stand up on the back of my neck as I breathe him in.

"No, I'm sorry, but I've gotta go. Crap."

"What's going on?"

"Chris, my son, he just got suspended from school. I've got to go pick him up. Is it alright if I go over the program with you later?"

"Yeah, sure. Of course." Mack waves his hands at me. "Go deal with your delinquent kid," I know he's joking, but the comment hits a bit too close to home. He has no way of knowing how much Chris has been acting out since Joel died. How he's fallen in with a crowd that keeps me up at night sick with worry. How I pray to God to show him the way out of this darkness before he ruins his life.

"Thanks, ok, I'll probably be back in a couple hours and we can go over it then." I start walking toward the door.

"No problem. Hey, if you need good old Captain America to do a public service talk with your boy, swing him by here sometime. I'll straighten him out for ya," he smiles.

I nod politely and bite my tongue. As I walk toward the door I don't tell Mack that a sit down with him might actually be the best thing for him. After all a heart-to-heart between a boy and his father can probably do a world more good than anything I can pass on to him.

Especially when his father is a famous, American war hero.

CHAPTER 11:

Year - 2014

Lauren

I pull into the school parking lot with my head buzzing like a beehive and my stomach filled with dread. This is the same elementary school that I went to when I was Chris's age. This is the school where I met Mack Forrester. Now his son is walking the same halls, charming some of the same teachers and stirring the same shit up as his dad.

Even if Joel hadn't died last year, Chris would still be a handful.

It's in his DNA as much as the almond skin tone he gets from me is, or the mischievous smile he gets from Mack.

Since the day he was born, Chris has always been a handful. I was blessed with the kid who climbed out of his crib and pulled the curtains down when he was one. The kid who decided the bathtub was an ideal place to put garden snakes when he was four. The boy who stole cardboard and other trash on garbage day for months so he could build a huge Evil Knievel style bike ramp across the street of our subdivision.

It was two days in the hospital getting his leg set and casted up for that one. And, of course, about a week after it was removed he built another ramp. This time it was sturdier and he landed the jump. He also got to spend almost an entire month in his room being proud of himself.

Even before Mack was all over the news, I never had a chance to forget him. Not when his son has been putting me through the paces, giving me no rest, and melting my heart with his father's signature smile.

Once Joel passed away, Chris spiraled out of control. Simple pranks and adventures took a darker turn toward destruction. He dropped out of almost all of his activities, giving up everything except football for a group of boys that look like a gang in training. All they're missing are little name tags. *Hello My Name is: Thug.*

Initially when Joel was killed in the accident, I took Chris to a psychologist who said that he'd stop acting out after six months or so. We just hit the anniversary of Joel's passing a few months ago and, if anything, Chris has only stepped up his efforts. I feel like he's an engine that's picking up steam on whatever this track is that he's decided to head down, and I'm left feebly standing at the end holding my arms out to try and stop him. But we both know he has the power to mow me down.

I make my way into the principal's office. A path I wish I couldn't sleep walk to. My son is sitting on a little plastic chair against the wall across from the school secretary, Miss Wilmot. I give him a look and as he tilts his head and peeks up at me from under the brim of his ball cap. He knows he's in shit, the flash of fear in his eyes doesn't escape me.

However, the older he gets, the more we're both coming to realize that a mother only has so much power. I can yell until I lose my voice, I can take away every single thing that he enjoys and ground him, but I can't seem to change this path he's on. He won't be happy until he watches his entire world go down in flames. He doesn't know yet how difficult it is to build a life from ashes.

Miss Wilmot looks over her glasses at me with a look that instantly transforms me back into a ten-year-old. My gut twists up into a knot and when I reach the edge of her desk I'm surprised that I don't have to stand on my tip-toes to look over at her. It's strange how a place or a moment can make us all children again. Like decades of growth haven't slid by us. Like our timelines shrivel down, depleting years of experiences with a single stare.

"Ms. Brickman, how nice to see you again. Too bad it's never under different circumstances." She looks over her wire-rimmed glasses and I stare down into my palms. How does she do that? I need to bring her to my house to give Chris that look when he's acting up. I'd most certainly have a much different son.

"Mr. Vaughn is waiting for you in his office, you can go right in." he continues.

"Thank you," I mutter, my ears burning up and the skin on the back of my neck prickling as I watch my feet shuffle to the office door. Put my hair in twists and my feet in Mary Janes because somehow the last eighteen years of my life have disappeared. I'm a butterfly who lost her wings, crawling into the office.

The door is open and Mr. Vaughn doesn't look up from the file folder he has under his nose when he waves me in. "Come in, come in. Sit down, sit down." he repeats himself.

I sit across the desk from him and fold my hands in my lap, waiting for him to stop reading whatever the folder holds. It's thick and tattered around the edges. Chris Brickman is written down the side tab. I swallow hard when I try to imagine how many offenses that folder must hold for it to be so thick.

"Ms. Brickman." I jump in the worn office chair as the principal jolts me from my thoughts. "As you can see, your son has had another incident here that we need to discuss." Mr. Vaughn carefully places the file folder on his desk and fans several sheets out across the top.

"What happened?" My mind races with possibilities. What have I already been in here for this year? Disrupting classes, fighting, skipping school, the list swirls through my mind as I wait for the next step in his delinquency to be reached.

"Christopher was found with explosives in the boy's bathroom today, Ms. Brickman. I'm afraid that between our zero tolerance policy on weapons at school and the damages that he and his friends did in the restroom, he's facing expulsion this time." Mr. Vaughn squints his already beady eyes at me, waiting for me to close the gaping hole my dropped jaw has left in my face.

"Explosives? Are you sure? I mean, I know you're sure, of course," I raise my hands like I'm trying to clutch my words from the air before they reach his large, flat ears. "I have no idea where he'd get them, I mean. Did they make a pipe bomb? Or maltov cocktail? Or …" I wrack my brain.

"Cherry bombs." Mr. Vaughn answers me matter-of-factly.

"Cherry bombs?" I parrot his words, but they don't match the pictures in my head. "That was the explosives?"

"Yes, Ms. Brickman. Christopher and a couple other students decided to drop a handful of lit cherry bombs into a student toilet this morning and blew it up."

"Blew it up? It exploded?" I try to imagine the scene. Are cherry bombs that powerful?

"Well, it blew the lid off the seat, yes. And it also made a terrible mess. There was water everywhere." His face flushes a deep maroon as he relives the horror.

"Cherry bombs." I sit up straighter in my chair, suddenly feeling my butterfly wings return once more as I transform back into the twenty-eight-year-old I am.

"Yes." Mr. Vaughn nods severely.

"Those were the explosives? So, Chris and his friends threw cherry bombs in a toilet and it blew water all over the floor?" The visions I had of shrapnel and smoldering tile laying in broken piles of the boy's washroom are replaced with the kind of innocent foolishness that boys do so often, even Bart Simpson has been immortalized doing it on the Cartoon Network.

"That's correct," the principal snaps at me. He points down to the many forms he fanned out in front of his folder. "As you can see, I have plenty of witness statements, including one from your son admitting that he was the one who brought the explosives to school today and that he participated in the destruction of school property." He taps his finger like he's trying to communicate in Morse code against the sheets.

"Ok, so, Chris and his friends pulled a prank with some cherry bombs and now he's getting expelled? Isn't that a bit much? I mean, boys do this kind of thing all the time don't they?"

"No, Ms. Brickman, boys don't. In fact, with only three months left of the school year there has been exactly one incident with explosives in the school ..."

"With cherry bombs, you mean?"

"Yes, with explosives. And it was Chris who incited it. If you'd like to take a look at his record, Ms. Brickman, you'll see that Chris is often the ringleader in such cases. As I said, there's a zero tolerance policy with weapons at this school."

"Cherry bombs." I repeat.

"Any weapons." he answers firmly. "Unfortunately, I can't extend Chris anymore chances. If his behavior wasn't getting progressively worse with each incident, then I could think about suspension. However, it's clear that he's not getting the guidance he needs outside of school hours in order to modify his behavior."

Well, that does it. "Listen, Mr. Vaughn. It's one thing to drag me in here from work and try to make my kid sound like he's a school shooter for throwing some cherry bombs in a toilet, ok? But, it's quite another when you decide to insinuate that I'm not pulling my weight as a mother. If you bothered to look at that file, you'd see that a little over a year ago, when my husband died, I became a single mother. I don't expect you to use that as an excuse for Chris, but it might explain his escalating behavior a bit. Maybe if you'd ever bothered to send him to the school counselor, you'd know that too. So, instead of sitting there judging my parenting skills, maybe you should be analyzing your supervising practices a bit." I stand up, breathing in deep into my lungs. My transformation back to adulthood is complete and I'm ready to take my kid and go. Enough of this garbage. I turn on my heel and head toward the office door when Mr. Vaughn clears his throat.

"Ms. Brickman, before you go, we need to discuss the matter of financial compensation for the damages."

So much for my dramatic exit.

CHAPTER 12:

Year - 2014

Lauren

"It's no big deal, Mom." Chris slumps into the passenger seat and buckles himself in. "Mr. Vaughn is such a dick. I mean, he's had it in for me all year just cause he caught me kissing Hannah. He's a total douche."

I don't disagree.

But that stays in my head. There's zero chance I'm sharing that information with my son. What I personally think about his principal doesn't change the fact that my kid is expelled from school and I have no where I can put him.

At nine, he's much too old for daycare and too young to legally look after himself. With only a few months left in the school year, there's no way I can just get him back on track in another school. We're basically screwed. I'm screwed on child care; Chris is screwed on having any hope of passing the fourth grade. What a mess.

Fucking Vaughn is a douche.

"Listen, I don't want to hear it. And don't you dare talk about your principal that way."

"Ex-principal," Chris corrects me.

Lord, give me the strength to keep my hands on the wheel so I don't smack my child. I know it's been nine years and I've never hit him, but I swear, I'm losing my patience.

"Do you think this is funny, Chris? Do you have any idea how badly you've messed this up? You're expelled, Christopher. That means I've got to try to figure out how I can get you back in school. In case you haven't noticed, I have a job I need to go to every day so I can keep food in your mouth, but now I've got to use my breaks to call around so I can get you back in class. And if that doesn't work, you can look forward to being the oldest kid in your fourth grade class next year!" The skin underneath my fingers pinch as I tighten my grip on the wheel.

I glance over at Chris, he's emotionless and staring out the window. I want to shake him and hug him at the same time. I want to soothe him and tell him I know how hard it's been for him since he lost his father.

Well, Joel wasn't his biological Dad, but Chris didn't know that. He was only two years old when Joel and I started dating. Joel had tried to pursue me before that, in his own awkward way. However, after spending the first year of my nursing program with a belly full of baby, I was in no hurry to find another man.

While the rest of the girls in my program were going out and getting drunk on the weekends, I was living with my Ma and big sister, studying from two types of books. Nursing text books and What to Expect in your pregnancy and beyond books.

The hard work and sacrifice paid off though, because I graduated the top of my class and had my little boy cheering me on at graduation.

When Joel and I both landed our first jobs fresh out of college at the same hospital, I started to see him in a different light. And I don't mean the nasty fluorescents that line the hospital halls either. He wasn't the most exciting guy, or the most handsome, but he was kind and respectful. He knew that Chris was Mack's boy, but he never treated him like anything other than a son.

When Chris turned three, we had a small wedding. Joel adopted Chris and it all felt so perfect at the time. Of course, six years ago, I had no way of knowing that Joel would be killed in a car accident and that Mack would move back to Colorado.

Maybe Ma can look after Chris while I get this shit sorted out with his school? I cringe to think of asking my fifty-six-year-old mother to look after the child who exhausts me in my twenties. My sister is still living with her though, so it's not like I'd be tossing her to the wolves. Besides, Chris could use the firm hand of guidance in his life that helped raise me.

Wait a minute.

"Who's Hannah?" The name my son dropped earlier finally bubbles up through my swamp of thoughts.

Chris looks across the car at me with Mack's signature smile pasted to his face. "She's, uh, Mr. Vaughn's daughter," he admits looking up at me from under the brim of his cap again.

I swallow my smile, I don't want to encourage him, but I know it's too late. A laugh bursts from my throat as I shake my head. If I don't laugh at this ridiculous hand I've been dealt, I'm gonna cry.

Like father, like son they say.

Lord, help me.

CHAPTER 13:

Year - 2014

Mack

"Ok, so don't forget you can't just stand still on this, but I also don't want you going into an all-out sprint right now either," Lauren's still lecturing me. She's been pretending that there's nothing between us except a nurse and patient relationship all morning.

What Ms. Professional doesn't realize is I've noticed as her gaze has licked every inch of my body. I caught how her eyes hovered over the bulge in my shorts. She might be doing a good job fooling the staff with her little show, but I lost my leg, not my eyesight. She'll have to do a lot better than that to pull the wool over these baby blues.

"Just a jog, I've got it." I interrupt and she gives me a sharp look. I know she hates me brushing her off like that, but I've been waiting a long damned time to get this carbon-fibre blade and I don't want to sit on the sidelines of the track listening to instructions on how to run.

I *know* how to run.

"Yes, just a jog." She answers sternly, double knotting the bright blue laces in her sneakers. "And I'll do this first lap with you, so you can tell me if you have any problems, ok?"

I hop off the bench and am surprised by the springy response of the blade. In that small movement, I already feel lighter and faster, and I haven't walked a step yet. "You got it." I throw three fingers up to my brow in a sloppy salute and her nose gets these cute little crinkles on it as she frowns at me. Her gloss covered bottom lip sticks out just a little in a tiny pout.

God, how I want to just pull that lip in between my teeth and give it a little nip. I want to feel the heat of her breath on my skin as I make her cry out my name. Somehow I manage to direct my gaze back to the track and decide I'll put this pent up energy into our little run instead of thinking about Lauren's sexy round ass that she's purposely showing off in a pair of skin tight yoga pants. Or her full, perky tits barely contained by her low cut tank top.

Like I said, she's not fooling me with her little act.

Even though I'm eager to get out for the first run on my blade, I fall behind Lauren, just a bit. I mean, there's no point in letting that sweet view go to waste now is there? When I left for the military, she was only a few months into adulthood. I remember her at eighteen, she was undeniably beautiful even if her body was still a bit lanky and a little awkward.

Now, at twenty-eight, she's a goddess. Her frame has filled out with curves that would make a priest snap his neck taking a second look. It makes it hard to concentrate when all I can think of is how much better we'd both be in bed now that we've got some experience behind us.

As we stand side-by-side on the track, Lauren twists her arms out behind her in the world's most unnecessary stretch. You know, you've really gotta limber up those shoulder muscles for a light jog. What's next? Some downward dog yoga poses? That's probably the most practical way to stretch her legs out, right? Regardless, I soak in the show she's putting on for me with her tits pushed out toward me as her back arches.

I'm not totally sure what her game is yet. It's clear to me that she wants me to notice her. And, well, she can check off that little box on the list. Done and done! On the other hand, she's been distant and cold with me. I can't decide if she wants to enjoy the chase, or if she still needs some space after losing her husband last year.

Enough racking my brain over it. If she wants me running around in circles for her while she gets some kind of kicks out of it, then she can get a taste of her own medicine right here on this track. "On your mark, get set, go!" I yell out and burst into a stride.

"Mack! I said a jog!" She yells behind me, annoyance dripping from her words. I hear her feet hitting the track not far behind me as she tries to keep up.

I love the crackle of the pine needles spread out over the track beneath me. My foot and my blade pound against the pavement, competing with my heart to see which can beat harder. The sweet smell of nature's decay reaches my nostrils, and I breathe it deep into my lungs. It reminds me that not all death is painful and horrible, sometimes it can be beautiful.

Suddenly Lauren pulls ahead of me, ripping me from my thoughts and giving me a new singular focus: *to win.*

Arms pumping at my sides, the muscles in my thighs twitch and pulse as I push myself to catch up. The cool spring air clouds my breath around me like a locomotive picking up steam as I reach her heels. There's no way I'm going to let her get past me that easy.

I've missed going for runs. I love how my focus narrows to one mission. The war, my men, my leg ... it's all miles away as my attention lasers down to the simplest of goals: run. It reminds me of the many mornings that Lauren and I would race each other for the last hundred yards of our walk to elementary school when we were kids. Our backpacks thumping against our backs, mud splattering against our shoes, despite our mother's warnings to stay tidy. Simplicity was the fabric of my life back then, patterned with rich colors and textured with deep emotions that all seem to drain away as we age.

Her spandex covered ass jiggles a little each time her feet hit the ground. It's hypnotic. I enjoy the view for a minute before pulling up beside her. She quickly looks over her shoulder at me and, I almost run out of breath. Not because I'm winded. But because, for the first time since I've seen her again, she's smiling. Her smile is like a radiant beacon of hope guiding me from the darkness. How did I ever walk away from that smile? One thing is certain, I won't be making that mistake again.

Lauren's focus returns to the track and I concentrate on trying to pull out ahead of her. I pull deep breaths into my lungs and dig deep to propel myself forward even faster. We're neck and neck, I can smell her on the wind.

BOOM!

The sound of an IED exploding fills the air and terror grips my heart. "Watch out!" Instinctively, I hurl myself at Lauren, tackling her to the ground and covering her with my body like a blanket.

"What the fuck!?" she screams as she thuds against the track.

I duck my head down beside hers, tucking my chin in against her shoulder and hold her tight. The track disappears and sand appears around me. I watch as metal fragments, dirt and body parts fly through the air around us as buzzing swarms my ears.

"Mack? Mack! MACK! What the hell are you doing?"

I blink slowly and the scene fades into the Colorado spring. The buzzing dies down and disappears, and instead I can hear birds chirping from the tree branches. Beneath me, Lauren looks like she can't decide if she's angry or scared. Her mouth is twisted up to the side but her eyes are open wide.

"Mack, what are you doing?" she asks again, but this time the fear is gone from her voice and instead there is a raspy tinge to her tone.

I realize that I'm lying on top of her, her legs are open around mine. Her tits are heaving against my chest. I can feel the heat from her pussy against my cock. Suddenly, Afghanistan feels like another lifetime.

"Sorry, I wiped out." I lie. "I guess I'm not ready for an all out race on this thing yet," I nod my head back toward my blade.

Lauren bites her lip and looks solemnly in my eyes, nodding slowly. I'm not sure if she buys my excuse, but right now I think she's a bit preoccupied. I can feel her heart beating wildly in her ribcage. She looks over my face like she's studying it, her eyes finally resting on my lips, like she's willing them to kiss her.

"That's ok," she murmurs. I feel her roll her hips up against mine, the movement is small, but undeniable. My cock throbs as blood rushes into it. She still hasn't made any effort to push me off of her or even to tell me to move.

I bring my face closer, hovering my lips over hers while I press my cock against her. She lets out a soft gasp and her eyes close. It's too much for me. I press my mouth into hers, kissing her urgently. My tongue traces her bottom lip and quickly finds hers. They barely have a chance to reunite when from the waistband on her yoga pants, I can feel a buzzing against my abs.

I pull back and glance down. Her phone. Fuck her phone. I want to pull her tank top down and lick her perfect tits until she quivers for me, begging me to make her mine. I want to fuck her tight little pussy again and push this stupid buzzing phone up against her clit until she comes.

"Mack, I've got to answer that. You've got to move." Her words are unconvincing, like she's asking me a question instead of making a demand.

"Are you sure?"

CHAPTER 14:

Year - 2014

Lauren

I'm *not* sure.

Of anything.

I'm not sure why I'm laying on the ground, wishing Mack would rip my clothes open and have his way with me in broad daylight. I'm not sure why I ended up here in the first place. I heard a car backfire and then it felt like Mack heaved me to the grass on the side of the track.

He said something about losing control on his blade, but I really want him to lose control of more than that. I want to feel the soft heat of his mouth taste every inch of my body. I want his lips back on mine. I want his fingers entwined with my own as the growing erection between his legs reminds me of what it feels like to be properly fucked.

His eyes have me locked in place. I wouldn't move, even if he wasn't lying on top of me. Even Joel never looked at me that way. Mack is the only man that has ever been able to make my skin raw and hungry to be touched.

My waistband starts vibrating again, like an angry bag of hornets that won't be ignored. My dreamlike fog erodes around me as reality snaps back into focus. I need to get up. I need to answer the phone. I need to get this session back on track.

"It's ringing again. I really need to answer it, Mack." My voice is clear this time as I regain my senses. He doesn't try to convince me otherwise. He never would. Instead, Mack rolls to the side and stands back up, extending his hand down to me to help me to my feet. Such a gentleman.

Sort of.

I brush the dirt and blades of grass off my ass and look up toward the hospital. I hope none of the other staff witnessed our little moment. I'm not sure I could ever explain it to anyone. I'm not even sure I can explain it to myself.

Mack smirks at me as I try to compose myself. "Don't worry, Lauren. No one saw anything," he answers my unasked question.

Even after all these years, it's like he can read my thoughts. "Besides, even if they did, just tell them I wiped out and had a hard time getting back up. No biggie," he shrugs nonchalantly.

My heart sinks a little at his indifference. I didn't expect Mack to stand up and profess his undying love for me or anything, but I thought that our kiss was more than "no biggie".

The persistent vibration of my cellphone against my stomach reminds me that I don't have time to stand here and over analyze what's happening between me and Mack. I pull the black phone out from the edge of my pants and see my sister, Chelsea, is calling. Before I have a chance to swipe my thumb across the screen and answer, the buzzing stops and her number disappears.

Suddenly the call history pops up on my screen and I see that she's already tried to get a hold of me five times in the past fifteen minutes. Wow. How did I miss that? That's the power Mack has always had over me, when he looks at me time erases itself from history. When he touches me, even if it's just from stumbling on his new running blade, the world and everyone in it ceases to exist.

Since we were just young and innocent children, I've been drawn to Mack like the ocean waves are drawn to the moon. Now that we're adults, those waves are quickly rising up into a tsunami, and I'm either going to be crushed by the force or swept away.

Bzzzzzz.

My hand trembles as my phone goes off again, shaking me back to the present. It's Chelsea again. Something serious is going on. I hope mom is ok! I swipe my screen and stick my finger against my ear so I can hear her clearly. Not that Mack is being noisy. He hasn't uttered a word. It's just that his very presence is distracting, so I need to give my senses a leg up.

"Hello?"

"Lauren? Oh, thank God I got you. I've been calling for almost twenty minutes!" She sounds breathless but the background is eerily quiet.

"Sorry, I couldn't answer before." I lie. "What's going on? Is mom ok?"

"Mom? Yeah, she's fine. No, it isn't mom. Listen, you've got to come home right now! It's Chris. No, don't come home. That's stupid, just go get him ..."

"Chris?" I almost forgot that I still need to spend my lunch hour trying to call around to see if I can get him placed in another school for the rest of the year. "Is he giving you guys a hard time? Tell him that I'm gonna put his bike on Craigslist if he doesn't behave. I'm tired of this nonsense with him."

He loves that bike. I always use it as my hail Mary when he gets too far out of control.

"Lauren! Listen to me! Chris took off with a couple of boys earlier. I told mom not to let him out of the house, but you know what she's like. As soon as I went to take a shower, she let him go."

Of course she did. Where was that soft touch when she was raising us? That woman had no problem introducing my butt to the flat side of her hairbrush when I got smart with her, but here she is letting my expelled son go out with his friends.

"Alright, do you know where he is? I'll call around and tell him to get his ass back there. He knows better than to pull a fast one like this." What am I going to do with him? Every day it seems like he's getting further out of my control.

"Yes, I know. Lauren, you need to leave work and go get him. The cops picked him up! Chris is in jail." Her voice cracks as my mind breaks into fragments.

"Jail?" The word barely comes out as a whisper, but Mack tilts his head and locks me with his eyes. "What do you mean he's in jail? He's nine years old! What the hell is going on?" I can feel myself losing my battle against composure.

"Lauren, I don't know what's going on. I just know that Chris left here with a group of boys a few hours ago. Then the cops called and said a parent needs to go pick him up. He's being held at the jail and they're looking at charges."

Charges? Jail? Chris isn't just spinning out of control. He's fucking spun out of orbit.

"I'll be right there. I'm leaving now."

Shit.

CHAPTER 15:

Year - 2014

Lauren

Chelsea was wrong about the location. Chris isn't serving hard time in prison. Not yet anyway. However, she wasn't wrong about the police picking him up. I pull into the Aurora police department and double check that I've got my wallet, keys and phone in my bag before I summon the courage to leave my car.

The officer on the phone wouldn't discuss what he'd been picked up for with me, she only instructed me to come down and get him. From her tone, I could tell that she probably thought I was some kind of stereotype. Just another black woman picking her son up from the cops. I can't help but wonder if my son wasn't black if I'd still be coming down here. I guess I'm about to find out what Chris did that was so terrible that they're holding a nine-year-old in custody. Part of me is already boiling up with indignant outrage, but another part keeps whispering: what if this isn't about the color of his hands, but whatever he did with them?

I nervously open the large double doors leading into the building and walk over to the Admissions Officer. She looks unimpressed as I make my way over to her station, greeting me with an arched eyebrow.

"Hi, I'm Chris Brickman's mother. I'm here to pick him up, please." I hold my purse strap on my shoulder to give my hands something to do.

The officer settles her blue eyes on me and her pale lips turn down. "I figured." She types something into the computer and then picks up her phone without uttering another word to me.

"Hey, yes, Ms. Brickman has showed up to pick up her boy. Ok, thanks." She drops the cradle back on the phone and keeps typing on her computer, without giving me another glance. "You can take a seat, Lieutenant Rogers will be out here in a sec," she waves her painted nails in the general direction of the chairs against the wall behind me.

I turn around and cross the floor. If this lady is any indication of what the cops are like at this station, then maybe my theory on why Chris got picked up is right. Before I make it to the tired

American Bad Boy

101

looking light blue seats under the window the door to the hallway opens.

Standing in the doorway is a thirty-something, black man with a shaved head and a strong jaw. He smiles at me, "Ms. Brickman? Come with me, please. Down this way," he guides me.

Maybe not.

Officer Rogers holds the door for me as I pass through, closing it carefully behind him. "Right this way," he holds out his hand like a signpost. "Now, Chris is sitting with my partner right now in another office," he walks slightly ahead of me and opens another door for me. This one leads into a small office decorated with little more than a desk and chairs. "But, before you go get him, I wanted to have a chance to talk to you about what happened today in private." Again, he holds his hand out, guiding me to a seat at the desk.

"Sure, ah, is he alright? I'm not even clear on what happened today." I ease back into the chair and watch Lieutenant Rogers as he sits down. He looks so relaxed, leaning back in his chair with his hands draped off the arms, I can feel my own anxieties melting away a little.

"Oh, he's fine. Not a scratch on him, don't worry about that. Now I can see that you've rushed over here from work," he nods at my exercise gear, "so I won't take up too much of your time. The reason Chris got detained today is because he and his friends decided to skip school today and vandalize the 7-11 on Havana street."

I don't tell him that Chris wasn't skipping class because he was already expelled. I don't think that will help anything.

"What did they do?" I cling to hope that "vandalism" means the same thing to this officer as it did to Chris's principal. Does my son just have a strange obsession with cherry bombing public restrooms?

"They swarmed the store at around 10:50 this morning, Chris and seven other boys, and they started ripping juices and milk out of the back fridges, smashing them on the floor. Chris ran down the aisle and cleared the racks of chips and junk, sweeping it all onto the floor. Then, when the other boys started to run off, Chris knocked over a newspaper rack into the store window, shattering it."

Okay, so not cherry bombs then. Holy shit. What is going on with him. I open my mouth, but my throat is a desert so all I can do is make a strange clicking sound.

Officer Rogers looks at me with sympathetic brown eyes, "I can see you're upset. This is probably a lot to take in. The thing is though, we caught all of the boys and questioned them here. It seemed pretty clear that Chris wasn't just following the crowd on this one, Ms. Brickman. From what we've gathered, this little operation was his idea and the other guys were following him. Even the store clerk mentioned that it was your son who broke the most stuff and then also took it upon himself to take out the window too."

I try to imagine Chris being so violent. Not only heading down a path of self destruction, but leading the pack. Instead, all I can think of is how only two years ago I had a sweet seven-year-old who still told me he loved me when I tucked him in at night. Now, I apparently have a nine-year-old delinquent going on twenty. More like, gonna get locked up for twenty, if I can't get him straightened out.

"I don't know what to say. This is, well, I knew he was getting out of control, but this is shocking." Tears build up in the corners of my eyes and blur my vision. I don't want to break down right now, but my throat burns as I struggle to keep them from falling.

"I can see that," the Lieutenant lifts a tissue from his Kleenex box on the desktop and hands it to me. I dab my eyes, sniffling. "Chris mentioned that his father died last year when we were talking to him. It's the only time he showed any emotions. I'd like to propose that Chris goes to a group therapy session in town here that's specifically for boys who are tweens and teens who've lost a parent. I think that it might do him a world of good to learn to cope with his emotions constructively, and see that he's not alone in grieving his loss."

"Is that expensive? I mean, I'll make it work, but I'm just not sure how ..." my thoughts begin to spiral as I start calculating how much I have on my line of credit.

"No, it will be free. I'm going to contact the program co-ordinator and recommend Chris to the sessions like a community service program. That way it won't cost you anything. Also, if you do agree to send him, I can use that as a deal to prevent the store owner from coming after you personally for damages."

"Me? Oh my God, I definitely don't have that kind of money." The very idea of being tied up in legal litigations makes my head feel like it's about to split open. "No, of course I do want him to go.

Even if it wasn't for the damages part. I just want him to get help." Tears roll down my cheeks and I quickly raise my hand to soak them up with the tissue.

"I can see that, Ms. Brickman. I think you'll find it will make a big difference. Chris is young and he's troubled but he has a mother who truly cares about him. I think with this group therapy, you'll see him turn around. He's already got a lot more going for him than almost every one of those kids he was vandalizing that store with this morning."

"Thank you, I do care," my voice cracks. "He's my world, I'll do whatever it takes to get him back on track. I swear to you, before his father died, Chris would never have even thought of doing stuff like this. Never. All he wanted to do is play sports, video games and normal kid stuff. Now the only sport he gives a crap about, sorry," I look up at him, but Officer Rogers just smiles back. "The only thing he still cares about is football, everything else is a wash. I just want my old kid back." I choke on my words as tears form again, but this time I can't hold them back. The dam breaks and a stream of sadness and worry flows down my face.

Lieutenant Rogers waits patiently for me to get myself back under control, handing me more tissues. Thankfully, after a few deep breaths, I manage to stop crying.

"Thank you," I mumble from behind a handful of crumpled Kleenex.

"Certainly," he answers with a friendly smile. "If you're ok, I can take you to the other office to pick up Chris now?" He doesn't stand up or try to rush me out of his office, even though I'm sure he has other things to do today. Instead, he waits for me to answer.

"Yes, thank you. I'd like to take him home now." I blow my nose and throw the tissues in the trash bin at the side of the desk.

"Great, ok, follow me. And remember, Ms. Brickman, your son is clearly dealing with a lot right now, but your little boy is still in there. Don't give up on him, take him to those sessions, I think you'll find the kid you miss before long." His looks at me softly and I swallow the lump in my throat before it has a chance to rise and spill over into another bout of crying.

"Thank you, Officer. I will."

"And you are going to march into your grandmother's house and apologize to her and your aunt for what you've put everyone through today. Do you understand me, Christopher?"

He shrugs without breaking his stare out the passenger window. The tears I spilled in the Lieutenant's office a few hours ago have long since been steamed away by my anger.

After spending the better part of my day at the police station, filling out forms for my son's upcoming group sessions and to get him released into my custody, I'm kinda over the crying thing.

I pull the car into my mother's driveway and throw the car in park. Chris doesn't move, still staring out his window.

"Let's go, young man! Now!" I bark at him, but he moves with sloth like speed to unfasten his seatbelt.

"Whatever."

I close my eyes and take a deep breath. I know he's testing me. I have no idea why, but it's clear as day that he is. Instead of giving him the reaction he's clearly searching for, I just leave the car and wait outside the door. I send a silent prayer up to God to give me the strength I need to deal with my boy.

Chris reluctantly joins me as I walk up the short path to my mother's front door. Before I have a chance to grab the handle, the door flies open with my sister, Chelsea standing in the doorway.

"Oh my goodness! Ma! It's Chris and Lauren. Are you alright, Chris? What happened, Lauren? I'm so glad you're home!" she rambles, blocking our entrance to the house.

"Everything is sorted out, for now. You wanna let us in?" I gently remind her to get out of the way. Chris, on the other hand, pushes past his aunt like a linebacker.

"Chris! Apologize to Chelsea right now. You don't push her around."

"Sorry," he rolls his eyes. I can feel heat rising up the back of my neck as I try to keep the flames of my temper extinguished.

My mother walks into the living room with us, with worry etched on her mahogany face. "Oh, Christopher! I'm so glad you're back. You gave me a real scare today. What were you thinking?"

Chris just shrugs, refusing to look any of us in the eyes.

"Apparently he was thinking that him and his friends should go trash a 7-11 for fun and the cops picked him up. They told me that if it wasn't for the minimum age for delinquency charges in

Colorado being ten, Chris would be looking at real charges right now. Luckily, they made us a deal so I won't have to pay for the damages he caused, like smashing out a window," my mother and sister gasp.

"Christopher!" Mom interrupts.

"Yeah, so if he goes to a group therapy thing in town, the police are going to kindly let it drop."

"Wow, Hun, what's going on in there?" Chelsea rubs his head affectionately.

"Leave me alone," Chris shoves her hand off his head.

"Christopher! Apologize right now." I barely grit the words through my teeth.

Chris sighs exaggeratedly, "Sorry. I'm soooo sorry. Sorry for being alive, ok? Is that what you want? Can you stop being such a bitch now?"

Rage prickles my skin and my mind flashes red. My open hand swats him on the back of the head and everyone stares in silence. I've never hit my son before. Never. It's the one thing I've never done.

"I hate you!" Chris's voice cracks and he flees the front door and stomps down the sidewalk to the car. The passenger door slams and I burst into tears.

"Hey, it's ok. I would've smacked him too with that mouth. He'll come around, don't beat yourself up," my mother wraps her arms around me and I cry into her shoulder.

I don't know what to do. It's like everyday that passes is just pushing more distance between me and my son. I don't even know him anymore.

I'm losing him.

CHAPTER 16:

Year - 2014

Mack

The stairwell echoes as I run up another flight at the hospital. With every step my prosthetic leg thuds against the concrete, despite my best efforts to hit it lightly. I want my feet to sound the same when I walk. I won't stop practicing until I can't hear the difference between them anymore. It's not because I'm ashamed.

Far from it.

I lost my leg so two men could live. I'd call that a fair trade. No, it's not shame. It's that I don't want anyone knowing that I have a prosthetic leg just by looking at me, or by listening to me. I don't want to deal with people's questions all the time. And even worse: their pity.

The muscle fibers in my ribs wrench angrily, making me stop dead in my tracks. When did I become such an old man? I throw my arms over my head and lean back against the cool wall closing my eyes. I remember when I first went to West Point, I could march ten miles with a sixty-pound ruck sack in the morning, hit up the gym in the afternoon and then stay up all night fucking the brains out of my flavor of the week. The energizer bunny was a pussy compared to me. Fuckin' pink rabbit.

Speaking of old men, I wonder how Cameron Armstrong is making out. When I went to Walter Reed to learn to function again, he made good on his word. He didn't renew his next military contract and went to Colorado University instead. When I was first learning how to walk with my prosthetic, Armstrong sent an e-mail my way. He thanked me for doing what I did and for saving his life. He let me know that he made it onto the Buffaloes as a quarterback. He even got kinda gushy at the end when he said he'd never had a brother, but that as far as he was concerned I was his brother, not just in arms, but blood.

His e-mail was kind, thoughtful and uncharacteristically vulnerable.

It pissed me the fuck off.

Instead of being happy to hear about him following his dreams, I was jealous. There I was, sweating my sack off trying to learn to walk like a damned toddler again, and he was set up to be the star of his college football team. Yeah, jealous doesn't really cover it.

I should really look him up now that I'm here. Let him know I'm happy for him.

I pop my eyes back open, dropping my arms back by my sides. Time to get back at it. I pull the air deep in my lungs and get mentally prepared to continue my run.

Thud!

A door opens into the stairwell a couple floors above me. I tilt my head and listen. Just because the door opened doesn't mean anyone's in here. Several floors above me I hear a huge sigh. So much for that theory.

Suddenly sniffles ring off the walls. It's a woman. At least I assume so, from the crying. Not to say I've never shed a tear or two, I'm well aware that men cry too. It just sounds different when it's a lady, that's all.

I guess that's the end of today's run. I should just head back down to the lobby exit and give this chick some privacy. I think about it, I have every intention of going, yet for some reason that's beyond me, I keep moving up the stairs.

Now, I'm no white knight. Sure, you might be inclined to think differently because of how I lost my leg. You'd be wrong. I've never been the kind of guy to swoop in and dry some girl's tears. Women cry too much and for too many reasons to get tangled up in that. Yet, I can't stop my legs from guiding me up toward the sound of her cries. Something about the noise tells me her tears are deeper than a bad day. Her sorrow sounds like it's rooted deep in her soul.

The space between us closes and her sobs shatter the quiet. The empty stairwell reverberates her pain from the walls. I come up around the last flight of stairs and my heart clenches in my chest.

It's Lauren.

I stop dead in my tracks and my chest feels like it's been hollowed out as I watch her. She's sitting, slumped against the door with her knees pulled up to her chest and her head lying against them like a pillow. She's got her arms wrapped around her legs in a hug she so clearly needs from someone.

From me.

She looks like someone who has lived two full lifetimes of pain and suffering. I'm not saying she looks old or haggard. Cause, damn it, I don't know a woman on this earth that is more radiant or sexy than she is. It's not at all that she's aged, it's that she's defeated. She's broken down. Stomped to the earth.

And it's all my fault.

"Lauren, I'm sorry."

As I close the final stairs between us, she looks up, startled. She wipes fat tears from her perfect face with her knuckles. I reach the landing and hold my hand open to her, to help her off the floor. Plan B is to sit next to her, if that's what she needs. Instead, she grabs my hand and springs from the floor like a jack-in-the-box as I give her a tug.

"You're sorry?" Her eyes travel over my face, searching for something. Maybe it's for a shred of sincerity. It's not like I've been very open with her since I showed up here. Maybe she's searching for more.

"I'm sorry. I never meant to make you cry." I brush the last of her tears away and cup her chin in my hand. She looks at my lips and it's all the invitation I need. I wrap one arm around her, pulling her tight to my body.

"Oh! Um …"

She doesn't get a chance to make actual words because I smother her sentence with my kiss. Tenderly, my lips find hers. I let my lips tell her everything. How much I've missed her. How much I need her. How sorry I am for breaking her heart. My lips spill all of my secrets, without ever speaking a word.

I feel the tension melt from her body as she sighs happily into my mouth. Our tongues gently collide and I run my hand up her back until I reach her hair. The rest of my body is coming alive from her kiss. Like she's breathing life back into the void she left in my soul. Of course, with the rest of my senses waking, the urge to make her cry out in a different way builds up in me.

I walk her back until she's pressed against the cold wall, without breaking our kiss. My hand slides down from her chin and I quickly reach up, under her uniform and unsnap her bra with one hand.

Haven't lost my touch.

Her breasts drop slightly under the weight of her heavy tits. I can't wait to run my tongue over her dark nipples and fuck her until the only thing she's crying out is my name.

"Wait, what are you doing?" Lauren squirms sideways from

beneath me, putting inches of space between us that feel like cold miles.

"I'm just trying to make you feel better. I want to say sorry for making you cry." I give her a smile and she pauses, like she's thinking about it.

Instead, she snakes her hands up under the back of her shirt and hooks her bra back up.

"What? Jesus, Mack, you can't fix everything with your dick you know." She smoothes her hands down over her shirt.

Ms. Professionalism is back. That cock-block.

"Are you sure? How about I give it my best shot? I bet I can make you happy for a while," I murmur and step toward her, trying to shake of Lauren's prim and proper act.

Just because it's been a decade since I've had her, doesn't mean I've forgotten her wild streak. I know it's not buried that deep beneath the surface. Besides, from what I saw in her tight, little spandex gear the other day at the track, her body has blossomed in ways that would really do that wild side some justice now. The memory of her curves makes me hungry for her.

"No. Mack, I'm being serious." She looks at me with her large brown eyes. I know she's trying to be stern with me, but it's just making me want her more.

"So am I."

"Listen, I'm not one of your bimbo fan-girls. I know you, the real you. At least, I used to." Her voice trails off sadly and her eyes soften. Lauren quickly composes herself though, throwing her shoulders back and jutting out her chin. "Anyway, I'm not even crying over you. You're such an ego maniac!" Her eyes snap back up at mine. This time they stop me dead. She's not screwing around.

"You weren't?" I step back and run my hand over the back of my neck. I guess it was presumptuous to think she's got nothing else going on besides thinking about me.

Lauren might be right about the fan club bimbos. It's hard to remember that you're not the center of everything when every chick you meet acts like you are.

"Then, what are you so upset about?" I take another step back, giving her the space she needs to talk and giving me the distance I need to concentrate on more than her round ass and her tight little

…

Focus!

Lauren looks up at me sideways, like she's not sure if she can trust me. Or maybe it's my intentions she's struggling with.

"I seriously want to know. Maybe I can help or something?"

She tilts her head and shrugs, and I don't think about running my tongue over the soft skin of her neck. Well, not for more than a second. Two seconds, tops.

"I don't know if you can," she talks to our feet. "It's Chris. He's completely out of control."

"Hold old is he?"

"Nine," she swallows hard.

"Nine." I'm no genius, but it doesn't take one to do that mental math. "Wow, you and Joel didn't waste anytime after I left, huh?"

Lauren looks at her hands and I realize that I'm making this about me.

Again.

"Never mind, sorry, that's none of my business. But, nine-year-old boys love to stir up shit. I can tell you that from experience."

Her full lips twist up for the first time since I've seen her. Her face lights up and almost knocks the wind from my lungs with a simple smile. "I remember."

"Yeah, well, so you know it's probably nothing. Normal guy stuff."

"No. It's more than that. He's on a path of self destruction, Mack. He was expelled from school and then the next day he was picked up by the police for trashing a convenience store with his friends. This isn't just normal boys will be boys type stuff anymore. He's turning into a criminal." Tears fall back down her cheeks as her chin quivers.

"Hey, hey, come here. It's ok," Lauren steps back against me and I wrap my arms around her. "It's ok. Let it out. You're dealing with a lot right now."

"I just don't know what to do anymore," she confesses as she nuzzles her face against my chest. I run my palm over her black hair and try to figure out how I can help.

"Bring him here."

"What? Why?" She looks into my eyes.

"Bring him here and I'll talk to him, man-to-man. Good ol' Captain America might not do much for you," I give her a wink, "but a lot of guys Chris's age think it's cool or I'm cool or whatever. I bet if I could chat with him, I can help. At least a little."

Lauren dries her tears and contemplates my offer. "That might not be a bad idea, actually," she admits.

"Yeah, every once and a while I have a good one." I give her a playful squeeze and she laughs.

"Ok. You know what, I will. I'll bring him tomorrow. It's not like he's in school or anything."

"Sounds good. That'll give me time to think about what to say to him."

"Ok. Thanks, Mack. I mean it. I think that you'll really help. But, even if it doesn't, I appreciate you stepping up like this."

Lauren steps up on her tip-toes and quickly pecks my cheek with an innocent kiss. Just as quickly, she steps back, opens the door and disappears through it.

"You're welcome," I whisper to the empty stairwell.

Lauren is right, she does know me. The real me. And I know her. She still has feelings for me. I know that's why she just smoke-bombed me. But, that's ok, because I still have feelings for her too.

And by feelings, I mean I love her.

CHAPTER 17:

Year - 2014

Lauren

"C'mon, Chris. Quit dragging your feet and get a move on." I call back over my shoulder. He's not too happy that I'm forcing him to come to work with me today. I told him I was gonna make him mop floors, not that he'll be meeting one of his heroes.

It was nice of Mack to offer to talk to him. I think Chris might actually listen to someone he admires so much. With all the media coverage Mack has gotten, I think Chris sees him as a bit of a father figure.

Little does he know.

My gut twists with guilt when I think about how I still need to figure out how to discuss that with Mack. After all, he has a right to know that Chris is his son. I just need things to calm down a bit first. It's hard to bring up his paternity in casual conversation. Between his son making me run off to get him out of trouble every five minutes, and Mack trying to make a move on me every five seconds …. Well, it makes it difficult to throw it in the mix.

"I'm coming, jeez, calm down." Chris sulks behind me.

That does it.

I whirl around on my heel with my finger already drawn like a cowboy at a quick draw. "Listen to me, young man. I'm not one of your little friends. You talk to me with respect, Christopher. If you want to keep pushing me, I swear, I'll have you scrubbing bed pans by the end of the day."

His eyes grow about two sizes bigger. He doesn't need to know I don't deal with bedpans at my job. "Now, stand up straight and get your attitude in check."

I wait for the smart remark, or the eye roll, or the sigh. My shoulders are so tense; I feel like a cat ready to pounce on a field mouse. However, Chris just nods at me, straightens up and walks beside me.

"Ok, let's go," he agrees, leaving me in far deeper shock than if he would've tried to curse at me again.

I might be surprised, but I'm not about to let him know. "That's right, let's go," I parrot his words and march my son into the hospital.

We make it all the way to the elevator and Chris still hasn't given me anymore flack. This has to be some kind of record.

When the elevator doors pop open on Mack's floor, I'm actually feeling something I haven't felt in a long time: optimism. It's a cautious optimism, but I'll take it over the bleeding-ulcer-worry I've been dealing with all week.

I guide my son, our son, to Mack's room with a little spring in my step. Maybe all of this was just the storm before the rainbow. Maybe Chris will go back to being the sweet kid I knew before Joel was taken away from us. Maybe … Mack's room is empty.

Of course it is.

My hopes begin to tumble like a tower of Jenga blocks. They're probably built on a foundation just as stable.

"Nurse Brickman, so nice to see you!"

I wheel around to the direction of Mack's familiar voice and my heart soars. I need to get off this emotional roller coaster. These two guys are killing me.

Chris turns around and a smile brighter than the North Star spreads over his face. "No way! Captain America? I mean, uh, Captain, uh, what's your real name again?"

Mack laughs and I can't help but smile. "You know, people have been calling me Captain America for so long now, I almost forgot it myself. The name's Forrester. Mack Forrester. You can call me

Mack, if you want." He extends his hand to Chris and I feel a swell of pride as I watch our boy try his best to return a manly handshake.

I look at the smile on Chris's face and over to the same one on Mack. Mirror images. The resemblance is so obvious; I can't help but wonder if Mack has connected the dots just by glancing at him.

"I'm Chris," our son shakes Mack's hand and lets go. For a second, neither of them talks. My heart is thudding hard as I wonder if they can see the features they share.

"It's nice to meet you. Your mother speaks very highly of you," Mack finally answers. I let out the breath I didn't realize I was holding.

Chris looks over at me and raises an eyebrow in silent skepticism.

"It's true," I manage to croak. Between the fear of Mack calling me out on paternity and the overwhelming joy of watching my guys meet for the first time, I'm barely keeping it together.

"So, Chris ..." Mack trails off like he's thinking it all through.

Here we go.

"Your mom has been putting me through the paces, teaching me how to use my new running blade. Would you like to come down to the track with me so I can show her how I'm kicking her physio program's ass?"

Chris snorts at Mack's language and I shoot his father a look.

"I mean its butt. Kicking its butt," Mack corrects himself and gives Chris a wink.

"I'd love to. Can I?" He looks over to me with his soulful eyes, giving me his best puppy dog stare.

"Yes, of course," I nod. I can't help but grin at how excited Chris is. If he wasn't already too cool for school, he'd probably be jumping up and down like a kid on a bouncy castle.

"Alright, let me get changed and grab my blade and we'll head out."

Obviously, Mack has a plan. I'm not sure what it is, but I trust him. It's nice to see Chris excited about something again. I let myself imagine a world where Chris and Mack get along like this all the time. A world where the smiles on our faces don't feel new anymore. A world where the three of us are together like this all of the time.

As a family.

CHAPTER 18:

Year - 2014

Mack

"You into track and field in school?" I ask Lauren's son as I sit on the bench and attach my blade.

"Nah, I used to but I don't anymore." he shrugs.

"Do you play any sports?" I secure the prosthesis and check it over.

"Yeah, I still play football a lot. I wanna get on the school team when I get to middle school. I'm pretty good," he says, proudly squaring his shoulders back in a move I've seen Lauren do a hundred times.

I've never had much experience with kids. When my brother, Ben, was killed in the attack on the twin towers, my chances of becoming an uncle died along with him. So, I wasn't sure how this was going to go today. However, talking with Chris is easy. Even though he's only nine, I feel like I'm chatting with an old friend. Something about the way he talks, it's familiar. I guess that's to be expected from Lauren's child though.

"I love football. What's your team? The Broncos?"

"Yeah, but I also like the Seahawks," his eyes shine.

"Well, ya got good taste then. Ok, so whaddya say you and I hit the track for a little race? I've gotta warn you, I'm not one of those guys that's going to go easy on you because of your age. I'd get prepared to eat a little dust," I throw a little smack talk his way.

"As if! Even if you didn't have that thing," he points to my blade, "I'd still beat someone as old as you!" And he chucks it right back. I like this kid.

"Christopher! Mack's, I mean, Captain Forrester's prosthetic isn't called 'that thing'. Don't be rude!" Lauren interrupts.

It gives me an excuse to stop and check her out. She's wearing spandex again, and I've been trying to keep my eyes off of her out of respect for her kid. But, damn, if her ass looked any better it would be art. I'd have to throw the boy some change for the bus so I could show her just how much I appreciate the masterpiece she is.

Focus.

Right. Track, Chris, race. I got this.

"Don't worry about it, Lauren. It doesn't matter what he calls it, because I'll still kick his ... butt in the race with it." I smirk at Chris and he's returning my smirk right back at me.

"Yeah, yeah. We'll see," he puffs out his chest and we walk up to the track.

Lauren stays on the bench, which is really for the best. It's always a constant struggle with my self-control to be around her. I don't know if it's the talk we had in the stairwell, or me hanging out with Chris, but with the way she's been looking at me.... Let's just say, my self control would be bleeding out in a shallow grave if her son wasn't here.

Chris and I take our positions, lining up beside each other on the asphalt. The kid's got confidence, I can see that. His swagger reminds me of myself at his age. I bet he's got all the girls on the school yard falling all over him. Well, he would if he didn't get kicked out of school.

"You ready?" I look over at him. He's got his game face on. He's been blessed with his mother's skin tone and the same stubborn look of determination she gets when she's trying to prove me wrong.

"You know it," he answers.

"Ok, we'll race to that oak tree. Sound good?" I point to the marker at the track's midpoint.

"Why don't we just do a full lap?"

You have to admire his bravado.

"I'll beat you going to the tree first, then, if you want a chance to redeem yourself, we can race as far as you want afterward. Ok?"

Chris rolls his eyes good naturedly. "Whatever, I'll wait for you at the tree then."

Yep, I really like this guy.

"We'll see. On your mark, get set, go!" I yell and we break into a sprint. Chris is out in front of me, pumping his arms and pushing hard.

I adjust my gait for the springy bounce of my blade. I'm still not totally used to it yet. The kid is fast; I'll give him that. But, I'm faster.

Sucking oxygen deep into my lungs, I propel myself forward until Chris and I are neck and neck. For a split second, it almost feels like neither of us are moving at all. We're perfectly in step beside each other, making it look like the world is rushing by us, instead of us rushing through it.

"Meep, meep!" I do my best roadrunner impression, like I used to back in my grade school days when I was about to make my opponent eat my dust. Not that someone Chris's age knows who the roadrunner is.

I pull forward and give everything I have to put some distance between us. Chris is right on my heel though. He's relentless. Someone has been taking their Flintstone vitamins.

With one last push, I manage to put about a foot of space between us and raise my arm in victory as I soar pat the oak tree. I did it! That was closer than I expected.

Chris and I slow our run into a slow jog, a speed walk, and finally a normal walking pace. I'm trying not to suck wind, meanwhile, Chris is completely fine. He's not even breathing hard.

"Ok, you got me," he smiles. "I can't believe you can run that fast with that thing. I mean, that prosthetic," he corrects himself.

"Yeah, once you learn how to use it, it's just as good as having both legs." I breathe in deep and try to slow my heart back down.

"But, wasn't it hard to learn how to use that? I mean, running again and all that?" He looks up at me from the side of his eye, like he's not sure if he should broach the subject.

I was hoping he would.

"It was, Chris. Probably one of the hardest things I've done in my life. Physically anyway," I add.

"How'd you get so fast on it? I really thought I had this in the bag." He looks me straight in the eye this time, more confident in his questions now.

"You know, it took a long time," I admit. "When I first lost my leg, I didn't even really want to walk again," I confess one of my darker moments to him.

"What? Why?"

"Cause, I was pissed off. I lost something that meant a lot to me and I was angry at the world that I could never get it back."

Chris nods silently and watches the track in front of us.

"But then, I saw some veterans who also lost limbs in the war. I saw some who had moved on and learned how to live again and I saw some who didn't. Let me tell you, the guys that didn't, well, they may have only lost a leg or an arm or something, but then they let the anger about it take the rest of them." I look over at Chris, he's still watching the track but I can tell he's listening to every word.

"They were still living and breathing, but they might as well have had tombstones hanging around their necks where their dog tags used to be. They let that anger kill them inside. So, I did my physio and trained and followed your mother's program here," I look up as we're approaching Lauren on the bench and smile her way. My heart speeds up again when she returns it.

"And now look at me. I'm kicking a nine-year-old's butt in a foot race." I grin at him.

He laughs and I hope my message got through. "Well, I don't know about that. But you did win. Barely." He smiles back.

As we close in on the bench, Lauren stands up to meet us. "What happened out there? I thought you were gonna win at first," she puts an arm around her son's shoulders and gives him a quick squeeze.

"Ahhh, he just got lucky," Chris brushes her off, but shoots his mom a grin.

Lauren looks so happy for once. It's radiating from her.

"That's not what it looked like from here," she points at the bench.

"He almost had me. Honestly, I had to really dig deep to push past him," I come to Chris's rescue. I don't want him leaving here with a bruised ego.

"See?" He looks up at Lauren, vindicated.

"Hey, Chris," I sit down on the bench to change my blade to my regular prosthetic. "I'd like to talk to you about something, if you don't mind." The kid sits down beside me on the bench as Lauren stands a few feet away.

"What's that?"

"Well, since you're the man of your house, I was hoping to talk to you about taking your mom on a date." I watch as his eyebrows shoot skyward. Hopefully the word "date" doesn't upset him.

"Oh?"

"Yeah, see the thing is, I have these tickets to the Buffaloes game this Saturday and I was wondering if you'd mind if I took her out. I mean, if you're interested, I have an extra couple tickets. You could come as our chaperone, if you want?"

"To the Buffaloes game?"

"Yeah, I've even got a ticket that you can bring a friend with, if you want."

Chris's face looks like he just got the best birthday and Christmas gift all rolled into one.

"Yeah! That would be awesome!" He jumps up, springing toward Lauren.

"Mom! Can we go? Can we?" He jumps from foot to foot and Lauren giggles.

"Yeah, we can go," she agrees and Chris gives a whoop, pumping his fist in the air. "But that extra ticket is going to go to Chelsea," she interrupts his dance. "You're still in trouble, so you won't be bringing any of your friends," she adds sternly.

"Ok, ok. But we can go, right?" He looks over at her and she nods back. "Thanks, Captain America! I mean, Mack," Chris smiles at me.

"No problem, kid."

With my blade changed we all head back to the hospital, but now Chris is practically bounding back to the front doors, leaving us in his dust.

"Hey, thanks a lot. I really appreciate it." Lauren gives my hand a quick squeeze and between that and her smile, it's all the thanks I need.

"I told you I'd help," I nod toward Chris.

"You're a man of your word," she looks at the ground, biting her perfect lip. God, I want to kiss her.

"Always," I answer. "So, uh, about the game on Saturday?"

"Yeah?" She looks up.

"What time do you wanna come pick me up?" I smirk.

Lauren laughs and it's an easy, happy sound that reminds me of a dream.

A dream come true.

CHAPTER 19:

Year - 2014

Lauren

"Woo! Go Buffaloes!" Chelsea screams with her hands cupped around her mouth like a bullhorn. The team can probably hear her, too. When Mack said he had tickets to the game, I didn't think he meant for seats that are practically on the field. We're sitting so close that we can not only hear every word of the coach cursing out his boys, but we can smell the gum he keeps snapping as he anxiously watches the plays.

Chris and Chelsea are on their tip-toes, even though there's no one in front of them to block their view. I've never seen them so excited! I knew my son loved football, but didn't realize that Chelsea was such a fan. With two minutes left in the game, they're watching the field, unblinking, so they don't miss a second.

I'm pressed up against Mack on the bench, and happy to stay here. Don't get me wrong, I'm just as red-blooded as every other American. I follow football and yell at my screen every Sunday, just like everyone else. However, right now, I'm a bit more interested in the sexy guy to my left.

I sneak a peek at Mack and let my eyes wander over his rugged features. His brown hair is tousled just like when we were kids. But that's where the similarities to the boy I once knew end. Sitting next to me, with tattoos sneaking out from under his white tee is a man. No question. My gaze falls down over his muscles and my mind wanders to how his hard body would feel against mine once I ripped that shirt off him. And those jeans. They'd have to go.

I glance back at his face and feel my cheeks run hot as Mack watches me, smirking. So much for a subtle glimpse.

"Are you bored with the game?" His voice is like velvet and makes me want to feel his arms around me as he whispers in my ear. "Or were you distracted by something?" His eyes twinkle mischievously. He knows damn well I was checking him out. He's loving this.

"No, I was, um," my mind races as I try to save some face here. I'll give Mack a lot of things, my body, my heart, my future, but I'll never give him the upper hand. "I was just going to ask you how you got tickets this good. These seats are amazing." I lie. Well, it's not a total lie. I mean, those thoughts have crossed my mind in the past five hours. Just not when he caught me eye-fucking him.

"Uh-huh. Tickets, huh? That's why you were undressing me with your eyes? More like you were wondering how you can get tickets, to the gun show." He lifts his arm, flexing his bicep jokingly. Even though he's just kidding around, I have to remind myself to slide my eyes back over to his face when I see his cut muscle flexing tight against his sleeve.

"Oh, give it up!" I nudge him with my elbow gently. "Not every look from a woman means she wants to sleep with you." Why are his lips so distracting? Is there no safe space on his face or body that I can rest my eyes anymore?

"Maybe not every woman, but you do." His smile broadens like he's just won the Super Bowl. God, he's so arrogant. God, he's so right.

"Seriously, how'd you get these seats? This is amazing," I sweep my hand out toward the field. I almost feel like, if I'm not careful, I might bump one of the players.

"I have my ways," he answers slyly. I bet he does. He probably got them from one of his little bimbos. Not that I care. Except, I do.

Luckily, with only forty seconds left on the clock, the Buffaloes score a touchdown and the crowd erupts into deafening madness. Somehow, above the cheering and yelling, I can still hear Chelsea freaking out.

I guess I made the right call inviting her.

Mack and I stand up and join the crowd in their riotous screams of joy. On the other side of me, my son is happily jumping like he's stolen a pogo stick from a small child.

"Did you see that, Mom?" he screams over the noise. "This is awesome!" It does my heart good to see him so happy. After the year we've had, I was starting to wonder if he'd ever be happy again.

Lieutenant Rogers did us a solid by getting him into that group therapy session. I took him to his first one on Thursday, and I feel like I'm already seeing a positive change in him. Between the therapy, and the way he and Mack have been bonding, I'm starting to settle into this once unfamiliar feeling of hope.

"I saw," I answer him, but he's already back to watching the field. With the clock counting down, it's obvious that the game is over, but Chris doesn't want to miss a nanosecond.

The timer erases numbers until it hits zero. The game is over, the Buffaloes won. This couldn't have been a better day. When Mack first talked to Chris about taking me on a date, I was a little annoyed at how he played his hand. Going through my son to get a date with me was a bit sneaky. Now, I could kiss him for having such a great idea. And kiss him for having such sexy lips, and eyes, and abs … My eyes snap back up to Mack and he's smiling down at me. Caught red-handed. Again! If I'm going to keep working with him at the hospital, I'm going to need to step up my game a bit.

"Ok, let's pack it in," I ignore Mack's knowing smile and direct my attention at Chris and my sister. "Traffic is going to be a nightmare, so we might as well make our way to the car." I gather up my water bottle and check to see if I'm leaving anything behind.

"Wait a sec," Mack puts his hand on my arm and a tingle shoots through my skin.

"What's going on?" His eyes stop me in my tracks though. His hypnotic blues are playing their old tricks on my body.

"You'll see," he nods over my head toward the field and I turn around. Running toward us with his helmet tucked under his arm is the quarterback of the Buffaloes. He looks familiar, but I can't place him.

"Mack! Hey man, good to see you again," he walks up to Mack and claps his shoulder.

"You too, Armstrong. Great game out there, man." Mack shakes the quarterback's hand.

Armstrong. That name rings a bell, wait, Cameron Armstrong? From our graduating class? Well somebody grew up!

I look over at my sister to give her a look. After all, Cameron Armstrong had once spent an entire afternoon trying to pick her up. Back then, with her being two years older than us and already graduated, it felt like she was practically old enough to be his mother. I remember she enjoyed the attention, but shocked the high school junior when she passed on his rare offer.

If Chelsea remembers any of this, it doesn't show on her face. In fact, the only thing that does show on her face is lust. She practically looks like a human emoji with large hearts for eyes.

"Hi, Chelsea." Cameron's voice cuts through to whatever planet she's on and she startles back into the moment.

"Hey," she looks at him, confused. Yeah, she doesn't remember him. But, obviously the same can't be said about him. I'll fill her in later.

"Hi, thanks for coming out today. Did you enjoy the game?" Cameron looks at Chris and I think there's a very real chance that his head might burst.

"It was awesome! You guys rocked. Oh my God, that last touchdown too, I couldn't believe it." Chris rattles on excitedly.

"Yeah, I was hoping we could make that work, but you never know. It's just as much luck as it is skill sometimes." Cameron looks at Chris and then over to me. "Hey, do you think it would be ok if I take Mack and, I'm sorry, what's your name?" He looks back at my son.

"Chris."

"If I take my old Captain here and Chris for a tour? I mean, if you'd be interested of course," he looks back at Chris and I can't guarantee he won't faint.

"Yes! Can I, Mom? Please?" His voice has a tinge of whininess to it, like a toddler begging for a cookie.

"Your old Captain?" I ask Cameron before answering Chris.

"Yeah, this guy led my platoon over in Afghanistan. Hell of a leader, as you all know," he looks over at Mack, who gives me a knowing look.

"See, I told you I had my ways to get these tickets," he puts the puzzle pieces into place for me. I find myself secretly relieved that it wasn't another one of his fan-girls throwing gifts at him in exchange for God-knows-what.

"Well, thank you both for serving our country," Chelsea interrupts and Cameron looks over at her. You can almost see the rest of the world disappear from their vision in the look they exchange. Jeez, get a room!

"Mom!" Chris pleads from my side.

"Yes, oh, yeah. Of course you can do a tour. Chelsea and I will meet you guys out in the car, ok?" I look over at Mack and he nods.

That's all Chris needs, he's on the field quicker than an Olympic sprinter having a false start during a race. "Awesome!" he cries out, excitement trembling through him.

"Ok, well, I guess I should go then," Cameron mumbles but his eyes still don't break contact with Chelsea's.

"Alright, thanks for doing this for us, man." Mack claps Cameron on the shoulder, bringing him back from whatever imaginary field of flowers him and my sister seem to be running through in their love struck gaze together.

"Yeah, ok." Cameron's eyes come back into focus and he looks over at my son. "Let's do this. I'll give you guys the grand tour."

"Cool!" Chris jumps from foot to foot.

"I'll, um, see you around." He looks back at Chelsea again and I want to gag. "I hope."

"You will," she assures.

"And, I'll see you later," Mack gives my hand a quick squeeze and it takes my breath away like he kissed me.

I watch as my son and his father walk across the field with the gridiron bad boy we went to high school with. It's amazing how a week can change everything. Last week, life couldn't look any bleaker than it did. Now, I feel like I have my son back, and possibly Mack back too.

I can't wait to see what next week will bring.

CHAPTER 20:

Year - 2014

Mack

"**A**nd that's pretty much it," Cameron walks us back out on the field. It's not like there's a lot of behind the scenes besides the locker room and the coach's office. "What do you think, Chris? You wanna play college ball one day?" Cameron scoops up a football from the abandoned mesh sack of them at the players' entrance to the field.

"For sure. I mean, first I want to make the middle school team though," Chris looks around the nearly empty stadium in awe.

"You're not in middle school yet? Man, how old are you? Someone's been eating their Wheaties!" Armstrong chuckles at his own joke and Chris looks up at him with question marks in his eyes. "Never mind," he mumbles, realizing the reference is lost on his young audience.

"I'm nine, in grade four. Well, I was in grade four anyway. Till I got kicked out of school."

"Kicked out? What for?" Armstrong was never one for turning down gossip. It's good to see some things don't change.

"I dunno, I set off some cherry bombs in the toilets and the principal freaked out." Chris shrugs.

"Well, that sounds like a dumb reason to get expelled, but I don't know much about that. I do know that you'll never play college ball if you don't get into middle school. Hey, you two want to toss the ball around a bit out here?" Armstrong holds the football up in his hand and Chris's eyes light up.

"Can we?"

"Yeah, man. Let's do it." Armstrong jogs about ten feet away and I do the same in the other direction until the three of us are in a triangle.

Cameron tosses the ball to Chris and he catches it effortlessly. "Great catch!" Cameron encourages him. Chris stands a little taller and chucks the ball my way.

I cradle the ball in my arms before tossing it back Cameron's way.

"Thanks. And, I know that I need to get back in school. I'm

gonna try not to mess it up when I get back in," Chris catches the ball.

"I had to go to some group thing for kids who lost their parents and they told me that I haven't had closure yet, or whatever. I dunno." Chris chucks the ball at me and looks at his feet. "I don't really know what they meant."

My hand freezes in mid-air with the ball in it and I look over at Cameron. I talked to him ahead of time about Chris's situation, so this isn't news to him, but he's not letting on.

"You lost your dad? I'm really sorry to hear that," I can hear that the sentiment is heartfelt.

"Yeah, I haven't said it yet, but I'm sorry you had to go through that shit," I agree. "That's an unfair hand you got dealt, Armstrong and I know how important it is to get closure though. Don't we?" I chuck the ball back at my old Corporal.

"Yeah, man. That's no lie." He nods.

"You know, when I first got back from the war, I was really struggling with closure too. I lost some great men over there. Men I'd trust with my life. I did trust them with my life, and I felt like I let them down when I stepped back on U.S. soil and they didn't." I confess and for a moment, no one remembers to pass the ball. Instead, Chris and Cameron simply listen respectfully.

"What did you do? To get closure, I mean?" Chris prods and I'm grateful for the interruption in where my dark thoughts were heading.

"Hmm? Oh, I visited their graves and talked to them," Chris looks at me like I just grew another head.

"What?" he sounds like he thinks I'm pulling his leg.

"No, really. I mean, it's not like I thought they would answer me. I'm not crazy," I try to explain, "I just needed to talk to them though. To tell them I was sorry I let them down and that I let their families down. I had to tell them how it was an honor to serve with them, and that I wouldn't forget them." My voice grows thick and I swallow hard, trying to push down the memory with it. "It really helped." I admit to the ground.

I look up and Armstrong is watching me closely. He seems to suddenly remember that he's still holding the ball and he throws it over to Chris. "You know what, man? I did the same thing."

"Really?" Chris looks at him, tilting his head.

"Yeah, I went to the grave of my old buddy. I had to say goodbye to him, you know? I wanted to let him know that I got out of the military and came here," he points to the empty seats surrounding us. "I don't know why, but it really worked. I felt peace after that. Like I was finally closing a door on that part of my life."

Chris looks at the ball in his hand, then at Armstrong and I. We've obviously given him something to chew on.

"I dunno if that would work for me," he talks to the football. Armstrong walks in toward Chris and I follow his lead. I clap my hand on the boy's back dragging him out of the dark place I can see him going to, like he just did for me.

"Hey, maybe talking to your dad at his grave won't be the way for you. I'm just saying it worked for me. You gotta do what feels right for you, ok?" I explain gently.

"It's true," Cameron interrupts, "whatever you've got to do, just get that closure though. It's the only way you can move on and keep living, man."

Chris nods, but doesn't respond. I wonder if it's because he can't trust his voice right now. I decide that's probably our cue to get going. Besides, the ladies are waiting in the car for us.

"We should probably get moving, Armstrong." I step out to shake his hand. "Thanks for this," We shake hands, the same hands we fought to save each other's lives with. The man who told me I was as good as a blood brother to him. Only now, I'm ready to hear it.

"Anytime, Captain." He smiles at me. "Hey, Chris," he looks over at Lauren's son, "you wanna keep that ball?"

That does it. Chris's crestfallen face forms back into the cheerful smile he had when we started this tour. Thank God. I didn't want to depress him. Just the opposite, really.

"Yeah? That would be cool. Thanks!" Chris clutches the football like he was just given a diamond.

"No problem. Just remember to keep working that arm, ok? And, no matter how you gotta do it, get that closure. You'll feel like you've been given a new life when you do." Cameron sticks out his hand to shake Chris's and I can't help but feel a strange twinge of pride when the boy returns the handshake.

"I will." From the look in his eyes, I think we've done some good for him today. At least, I hope we have. He looks determined, maybe this is what he needed to turn a new leaf. No child deserves the tragedy and upheaval that Chris has had to deal with. I hope that this is the beginning of being able to put it behind him.

And I find myself hoping that I'll be able to keep being there for him, helping to guide him through it in the future.

CHAPTER 21:

Year – 2014

Lauren

"Do you remember that Halloween when my father caught you and your friends trying to t.p. my house?" Heat flushes through my cheeks as I laugh at the memory. Of course, the diminishing bottle of wine sitting on the coffee table probably has something to do with it.

"Oh, man. How could I forget? Your dad was so pissed. I thought he was gonna hand me my ass in a sling." Mack's eyes twinkle as he throws his head back and laughs. "I would've deserved it though."

"Nah, his bark was worse than his bite, but yeah, he caught you red handed."

"We were so dumb about it too," he runs his palm over his beard, "I mean, we had a laundry basket of toilet paper." He shakes his head and then takes another sip of the white wine we're polishing off.

After they finally came out to the car, Chris and Mack were joking around like lifelong friends. It did my heart good to see my boy so relaxed and happy again. I guess none of us were in a hurry to say goodbye. After Mack agreed to come over for dinner, him and Chris went outside and tossed the Frisbee around until the night sky grew chilly. Then they decided to warm up a bit by playing video games, talking smack the whole time. I swear, for a couple of hours, I wasn't sure if I had one kid or two.

Chris went to bed hours ago, but Mack and I are still up, basking in the glow of our sentimentality. That glow burns a lot brighter when you pop the cork on the third bottle of chardonnay.

"I still remember what he said, too," Mack continues. He puts his glass down on the table and straightens up as he imitates my father's posture. "One of you boys better have a serious bowel problem," Mack drops his voice like dad's signature baritone. "Because if I find you throwing that toilet paper on my property, you're gonna need every single sheet when I beat the shit out of each of you."

Laughter rises up from my belly like bubbles in a glass of champagne. It's nice to be able to laugh over memories of dad now. When the heart attack first took him, every thought of him stung. Actually, it feels good to let loose and laugh about anything again. With the year I've had, I was beginning to forget what feeling anything was like. Unless you count numbness and exhaustion. I was starting to believe those would be the only sensations I would ever have again.

"That was dad," I smile and hold my glass up in the air, "bless his soul." Mack closes his eyes and nods in a silent blessing. "Why were you trying to t.p. my house anyway? We were friends for a while by that point."

"Oh, I don't know. I was young and didn't know how to talk about feelings and stuff back then. I guess some things never change, huh?" He looks over at me and winks.

Mack is many things, but an open book isn't one of them.

"What were we," he continues, "Chris's age?" He slides his hand over my shoulders casually and resting my head against the crook of his arm feels like home.

"Yep, I'd say we were right around there," I agree. Sitting back up, I swallow the last mouthful of my wine and put the glass down on the table. I quickly snuggle back against him, breathing in his scent shamelessly.

"I guess it's probably because I loved you even then, but I didn't know how to tell you." His voice drops, but every word is etched into my eardrums and tattooed onto my heart.

Love me, even then? Does that mean he still...? I look into Mack's face searching for meaning in the words he hasn't spoken.

"Should I call you a cab soon? I don't want my co-workers wagging their tongues about having you out all night," I look over at the clock. It's probably already too late for that, but him staying the night certainly won't help.

"Why would they gossip about me being with you? Don't you know I went to visit my great-aunt Mildred for the weekend? You'd love her, she's such a sweetheart," his eyes glint mischievously.

"Mildred? You don't have a... oh, I get it," I have a bimbo moment. I'm not sure if it's because of the wine or if looking at Mack is distracting me. That's not true. I know what's clouding my head, not to mention my judgement, and it ain't the chardonnay.

He's gorgeous. I can't pry my eyes off his blues. With a few drinks in him, they're the color of a crisp autumn sky. Like a tumbling red maple leaf, I'm being tossed around, trusting him to safely place me on solid ground.

"Well, you can stay here then," I look down at his lips. Why are they so damned distracting? "But, you're gonna need to crash on the couch. I don't want to confuse Chris." I tell him honestly.

"I can respect that."

His broad hand slides over the side of my face and under my chin. My heartbeat quickens as my eyes travel down to his pink lips. Suddenly, those perfect lips are crushing mine in a bruising kiss. I can feel the urgency of his desire and the longing on his tongue.

Can he feel how my body craves him?
How my soul aches for him?
How my heart beats his name?

EDDIE CLEVELAND

CHAPTER 22:

Year — 2014

Lauren

Mack kisses a trail of burning desire down the tender spot on my neck. I close my eyes, making the heat from his lips build an electric buzz in my body. Each kiss sends pulses of electricity to my nipples, then down to my belly and it spreads down further, blossoming between my legs.

Damn, only Mack could make me so wet from a kiss. A simple

kiss was all it ever took to make me crazy. I've never been able to resist his lips.

"I can't wait to taste every single inch of you," Mack growls. I can feel his teeth graze my neck and a little shiver runs down my spine.

"Every inch, huh?" I smirk at the idea. A girl could do worse than having Mack "Captain America" Forrester worshipping her body. I doubt she could ever do better actually.

"Every inch," he continues kissing down along my collar bone, his fingers sliding up under the hem of my shirt. "From here," his fingertip grazes over my bra and I press my breasts against him, greedy for more. "All the way to here," he drags his hand down over my belly, over my ass and down my legs to my ankles. "Do you think I'm forgetting anywhere?" he teases me and my pussy clenches tight with anticipation.

"Maybe," I breathe.

"How about here," his fingers softly make their way back up my leg and stop between my thighs. "I'm gonna love eating your sweet pussy, Lauren." Mack gives me a quick kiss on my neck and starts tugging my shirt up over my belly to free me. But my body seems to have other plans.

Please, not now.

"Uh, Mack?" I creak.

"Yeah?" He pulls my shirt up over my breasts, exposing my lavender bra.

"I, uh, I've had too much wine. I need to use the washroom." I squirm, hating my pathetic bladder right now. Worst timing ever.

Mack sits back and looks up at me, "God, Lauren, you look horrified," he smirks. "It's no biggie, go pee. I'm not going anywhere." He sits back into the couch looking like he's been sitting on it since the day I bought it. He looks so perfectly comfortable in my home, like he's always been there. Like he always will be.

"I'm not horrified," I lie. "I just didn't want to ruin the mood."

Mack suddenly grabs my hand and pulls it between his legs, resting it on his hard cock pressing against his fly. I gasp, but don't try to pull it back.

"See? You couldn't possibly ruin the mood. Now go, hurry back."

Reluctantly, I pull my hand back and get my feet under me. Seriously hating my bladder even more after that. Damn, it seems like his muscles, tattoos and ego aren't the only things that've grown. His cock is hard, heavy and huge!

I scurry over to the stairs and jump up them like a gazelle, two at a time. I think I hear Mack laughing at me from the living room, but I hurry into the bathroom too quickly to say for sure.

Still cursing the wine and my bladder, I sit down and pee as fast as I can. With the toilet still flushing, I rinse my hands and see myself in the mirror for the first time tonight. I look ten years younger! I can't believe how much youth has returned to my eyes, I can't help but smile at my reflection. Mack isn't just good for my body, he's good for my soul. And my soul doesn't want to waste another second staring at myself in the mirror.

Heading out the door, I start for the stairs but stop in my tracks. I should check in on Chris first. It's not like when he was a baby and I used to stand over his crib watching him sleep. However, this has been a difficult time for him the past few weeks. I mean, seeing just tiny glimpses of my old son peaking through from behind the tumultuous clouds of pain he's been hiding behind for a year has given my heart so much hope. I just pray that it lasts. I pad lightly down the hall and sneak a quick look in his room. It takes a second for my eyes to adjust to the darkness of his space as I search for his bed ... it's empty!

Wait, where is he? I look around his room, snapping my head around so fast that it hurts my neck. He's not there. I flip on his light, "Chris? Chris!" No answer. Instead, his window is gaping open, like a mouth trying to shout the answers to where my son went.

His room is empty.

Cold fear spreads through my stomach as I turn on my heel and run to my room in search of my son. Flicking the switch to my light, it's clear that he hasn't been in my room at all, let alone to sleep.

"Chris?" My voice is rising with the panic rising in my chest. Lord, where is he?

I thump back down the stairs, and stop at the bottom. Mack is standing over by the mantle looking at our family photos. One family photo in particular. The large double framed collage of pictures showing the early years of my time with Chris. There is photo after photo of only my son and I at the park, on birthdays, Christmases, just enjoying life together. Just the two of us. That's how it was until he was three. Mack's eyes slide over to the next frame, the picture of my wedding day, where Joel, Chris and I are smiling at the camera broadly. I remember feeling relieved when Joel and I got married. Relieved that he was a good man who wanted to take Chris and I on. Who wanted to look after us, care for us.

I don't have time to wonder if Mack is putting the story together. I don't have time to explain that Joel is absent from years' worth of pictures because he wasn't in our lives then. I don't have time because right now, his son is missing and we need to find him.

"Mack!" His head snaps up at the edge in my tone.

"Sorry, I was just looking around a bit," he starts to explain.

"That's fine," I hold out my hand to stop him from explaining. I don't really care right now. "Mack, we need to call the cops! Chris is gone. Oh my God, it's almost midnight! Where could he be? Oh my God!" Tears swell up in the corners of my eyes.

"Are you sure?" Mack doesn't wait for me to answer, he lunges up the stairs and I can hear his prosthetic thump against the floor above as he searches the rooms.

I grab the phone wondering if I should call the police department or 9-1-1. I can hear Mack rush back down the stairs and close the distance between us.

"Lauren! Where is Joel buried?" Mack interrupts my disjointed thoughts.

"What?" My mind can't process his words. They don't make sense to me. I don't care about Joel right now; I want to find Chris. "What are you talking about?"

"I know where he is, I'm going to go get him, ok? Tell me, please, where is Joel buried?" Mack lays a hand on my shoulder and it's heavy. It brings me back from the edge. It calms me.

The grave is on Magnolia Lane, it's only five blocks north. At the Lewis cemetery. You think he's there? Why?"

"I know he is. Stay here in case he comes back, ok? I'm going to go get him. I promise. If he's not there then I'll call you, but I think he is." Mack gives out his orders as he grabs his things and heads out the door. Once a soldier always a soldier.

"Ok, Mack, are you sure? I think I should call the police. What if something happened to him." The tears spill over and wet my face, but I don't care.

"Hey," Mack grabs my shoulders and looks down into my face, "I told you, I promise I'll get him. Ok? You can trust my word, you know that. Please, try to calm down a little and I'll be back soon. I'll take care of this. I promise." He stresses and somehow it actually does slow my heartbeat a little from the borderline heart attack I'm having.

"Ok," I answer and Mack gives me a quick peck on the forehead and disappears out the front door.

"I love you," I whisper to the door shutting in my face. Please, Lord, let him bring back my baby. Please, let this all be ok.

CHAPTER 23:

Year - 2014

Mack

The pavement is thudding under my prosthetic as I run toward where Lauren told me the graveyard is. The cool air is rushing past my ears and I sweep my head from side to side for the first signs of the cemetery. I didn't have time to get detailed directions from Lauren. I could've brought her with me, but I feel like if Chris is there, and I expect he is, then he's not going to want to talk to his Mom. He needs his Dad.

Before Lauren came down the stairs, those pictures of her family … is Chris mine? When Lauren told me how old he was, I figured that she shacked up with Joel Brickman shortly after I left for West Point. Yet, I looked through a bunch of pictures of her and Chris by themselves for years. I mean, someone must have been taking all those shots, but it seems weird that Joel isn't in a single one until the wedding picture.

My eyes try to squeeze shut with the wave of guilt washing over me. I should've been there for her. Not Joel fucking Brickman. God rest his soul.

Running up the street isn't as easy without my blade. I've gotten so used to it now that I've been doing daily jogs and sprints. However, I can see the steel gate leading to the Lewis cemetery up ahead. I don't need a blade; I need to get … *my* son.

Is he my son? Why would Lauren keep that from me? Was she that angry at me for going to West Point? They say hell hath no fury like a woman scorned, but that seems ridiculous.

I should've been there for her.

You have no one to be angry at but yourself.

I slow my jog to a walk and stride in through the gate, searching the rows of headstones like and owl scanning a field for mice. Where is he? I don't see him anywhere. Just hundreds of grave markers shining under the moonlight. Some covered in fresh flowers from loved ones who still ache for their losses. Some long forgotten, their headstones crumbling and neglected.

I stop and tilt my head to listen carefully. All I can hear is the faded noise of traffic a few streets over. Maybe I was wrong. Maybe Chris didn't come here. Maybe I'm wrong about everything. He might not even be my kid.

The pictures on the mantle flash in my mind, the only thing is, Chris didn't look like Joel as a toddler. He didn't look like Lauren either except for her beautiful skin tone. No. He looked like me.

A small movement catches my peripheral vision and I snap my head over to investigate further. Almost twenty rows away I can see a small figure in the shadows. It's him. He did come here! I wonder what else I'm right about?

I want to yell his name, but I stop myself. What if he runs? Or I scare him? It's probably better to just go talk to him. I walk up the end of the row, so I don't trample on anyone's graves, and close the yards between us.

With each step I get closer to him, the more I'm sure it is Chris. I can hear his voice being carried by the night air. "Need to let you go …" He's sitting at the foot of the grave, talking to Joel. Just like Armstrong and I had suggested. I'm happy that he's getting the closure he needs; I just wish he would've waited until tomorrow to do it.

I slow down, I'm not trying to sneak up on him, but I don't want to interrupt him either. His back is to me, but I can hear the tears he's choking back in his voice.

"Mom and I are doing ok. I mean, it's been hard without you, real hard. I've been messing up a lot. I just get so mad sometimes that you're gone, you know? Like, why did you have to leave us when we still needed you here?" his voice cracks.

I stop a couple a rows away from him and let him speak his mind. I've been where he is and I know how important it is to say your piece to get some peace.

"It's been hard on mom." He sounds like he's accusing Joel angrily. "And, well, I've been hard on her too. I got expelled and then the cops picked me up. I know I'm making her worry. I just, I dunno, I just keep getting so pissed off. I mean angry," he sounds defeated and I watch as his shoulders slump forward.

"But I think things are going to get better now. Mom has a cool friend. You'd like him, he talked to me about you and stuff. Everyone keeps talking about closure and I guess it's important. That's why I'm here. I wanted to tell you that I still miss you and think about you all the time, but I don't want to be mad about it anymore. I want to go back to having some fun and doing stuff I like again. I guess I felt like I shouldn't be having any fun without you, but I know you wouldn't want that. So, I still love you, and I still miss you, but I'm gonna move on. I have to. I don't want to be mad all the time anymore." His voice breaks and so does my heart. Chris drops his head into his hands and his back rises and falls with his cries.

I walk over to him and he turns around quickly, wiping the tears from his face.

"Hey man, are you ok?" I look down at his tear streaked cheeks and wish I could do or say something that would take away his pain. I know from experience that the only true bandage is time.

"Yeah," Chris sniffs and swallows hard. "I just needed closure. Like you guys said."

I nod. I know he did. "That's all right, you did what you had to do. I understand that. Your mom is a bit worried though. She thinks you snuck out to run away or something."

I watch as his shoulders slump back down and he looks at his hands. "I messed up again, didn't I?" He sneaks a look up at me sideways.

"Nah, you did what you had to do. I'll explain it to her. I get it." I answer honestly. It's not a lie. When I decided to go visit Corporal Thompson's gravesite, I pulled a U-turn in the middle of rush hour traffic to do it. Sometimes things can't wait until morning, or for traffic lights. When your soul tells you that it's ready to heal, you listen.

"I'm just gonna give her a quick call so she doesn't keep worrying, ok? I'll let you finish up here." I pull my cell out of my pocket and Chris nods at me.

I dial the only number that I've bothered to program into this thing and Lauren picks up on the first ring.

"Hello?" I can tell from her voice that Chris isn't the only one who's been crying.

"Hey, I'm here with Chris. He's ok. He just needed to get some closure with Joel, but everything is ok." I soothe her.

"Oh thank God! I swear every time I think he's turning a corner he goes and does something like this! What was he thinking

sneaking off in the middle of the night! Thank you Lord, he's safe."
I can practically hear her crossing herself.

"He's not doing it to act out, ok? Trust me, it's a good thing that he came here tonight. He needed to talk to Joel as a man. It's because of me and Armstrong that he even got the idea, so please, cut him some slack this time? I don't think he's sliding back." I plead his case.

The phone is silent. I flick my hand over to check if the timer is still counting the seconds. It is.

"Lauren?"

"Ok," she finally answers quietly. "But he still has to know that leaving in the middle of the night isn't ok. Even if it's to go to the grave." I can hear the edge creeping back into her tone. I don't think she knows if she's relieved, happy, or pissed off. Probably all three. And then some.

"He knows," I interrupt gently. "Trust me."

"Ok, well you two get back here soon."

"We will see you in a bit." I hang up and walk over to Chris. He's standing up now and has wiped away the last remnants of his tears.

"Is she mad at me?" He looks up into my face and it's like looking back in time down into my own reflection.

"Nah. I mean, she was worried, of course. Don't worry, it's all gonna be ok." I throw my arm around his shoulder and give him a quick squeeze. To my surprise, Chris throws both his arms around me and buries his face into my arm.

"Thank you for helping me," he mumbles. "Not just with this, like, with understanding me, I guess." He lets go and looks down at his feet.

"Hey, anytime. Ok? I'm always here if you need me."

Chris looks up at me, his brown eyes searching my face. Like he's not sure if I'm just saying the words or if I mean them. He seems to find the honesty he's looking for, because his lips spread into a smile and he nods at me.

"Ok, let's go back to my house," he walks away from Joel's grave. "I'm ready now."

"Ok."

The only sound in the air is our footsteps as we walk side-by-side to the cemetery gate. I feel ten pounds lighter just knowing how much baggage the little man at my side just left back there. I can't even imagine how much better he must feel. Or how much better his life is going to get now that he's closing the door on his grief. I'm not saying it'll be perfect, but it should get easier now.

I look over the headstones, lined up like men on parade. All standing at attention, decorated and shining. My skin prickles and a rush of air whooshes in my ears as my mind travels back to the military gravesite I visited with my men lying in it.

The men I lost that day.

The men I let down.

Suddenly, my throat closes and I gasp for breath as I see Thompson's face in my mind's eye. Chris fades away, the stones around me disappear as I see the Afghani elder just steps away from me. His hand is hidden beneath his clothes, but I know what's there. I've seen this happen a million times. He pulls out his ax and the sickening thud is all I can hear as Thompson's head slices in half. The blood drips down what's left of his face and is soaked up by the sand billowing around us as he crumples in the dirt.

"Corporal!"

"Hey, what's going on? Are you ok?" I blink my eyes, covered in cold sweat and watch as Chris reappears. The dusty hell hole that I fought in quickly evaporates around me and the cemetery returns.

Chris looks frightened. I fight the urge to puke and wipe the beads of sweat from my forehead, my mind scurrying for some kind of answer to give him.

"Yeah, sorry. I think I might be coming down with something. It's late. How about we get you home so we can both get some sleep, huh?" My throat is dry as I manage to reassure him. The last thing I need is to have Chris and Lauren worrying about me. It's my job to look after them, not the other way around.

"Oh, ok," he looks like he's not fully buying it. At least he doesn't keep pushing it though.

What was I saying about leaving that baggage behind at the grave?

Let's hope it works better for Chris than it did for me.

CHAPTER 24:

Year - 2014

Lauren

The front door opens and I stop pacing and watch as Chris walks into the house with Mack behind him. I can't even feel my feet hit the floor as I run across it. I throw my arms around Chris and thank God silently.

"I was so worried!" My voice is hoarse from crying. "Don't ever do that to me again," I step back and hold my son by his shoulders. He looks up at me with soft eyes and a trembling chin.

"I won't, Mom. I'm sorry." I can see he's trying to keep it together in front of Mack. He probably doesn't want to cry in front of his hero. I won't put him through that.

"Go on up to bed, I'm gonna come up in a second," I give him another quick hug.

"Ok," he answers timidly. "Goodnight," he looks over his shoulder at Mack and then flees up the stairs.

"Did you talk to him? Did you tell him he can't do this to me?" I stare into Mack's eyes once Chris is out of earshot.

"I did. Lauren, I know you're upset ..."

"You're damned right I'm upset. Anything could have happened to him. Anything! He could've gotten hit by a car, or taken by a creep, I could've lost him, Mack." A sob chokes out my words and I cry into my hands. I feel Mack's arms around me, strong arms that feel like a brick wall surrounding me. I feel so safe with him. I always have.

"He's alright. I know he scared you, but I'm partly to blame for that. Cameron and I talked to him about getting closure by talking to people we've lost at their graves. I didn't think he'd sneak out tonight to do it, but I understand it. He had a lot to get off his chest. You've got a great kid there, Lauren. Go easy on him," his voice rumbles in his chest.

With my ear pressed against it I can hear his heart beating and his lungs breathing and his voice soothing my fears. Somehow, even just listening to Mack's body serving the most basic of functions, keeping him alive, calms my frayed nerves and makes me want to stay in his arms forever.

"I have to go talk to him," I murmur into his shirt, but instead of walking away I wrap my arms around Mack's waist. Everything feels so far away. The pain of losing Joel. The heartache of watching Chris lash out. My job. The world. It's all so distant as I just listen to Mack's heart.

"Of course, that's because you're a great Mom, Lauren. Go ahead, just remember that he's still fragile."

"I know." It's true. My son has become the king of cool in the last year, never shedding a tear, always ready with a smart remark. I could see how close to the surface his emotions were when he walked in. "I'll be back in a bit. I'm just gonna say goodnight to him." I manage to drop my arms from Mack's waist and my eyes flutter closed as he leans over me and softly kisses my forehead.

"I would expect nothing less," he smiles down at me and lets me go. Instantly the agony of the world feels closer. I feel less protected from it all. Like a wound with a band aid ripped off too soon. A shiver runs through me and I rub my hands down my arms.

"I'll be right back. Thank you for bringing him home." I kiss Mack quickly and then run up the stairs before my body has a chance to destroy what's left of my rational brain with it's desires.

I rap my knuckles lightly on Chris's open door, he's still awake.

"Hey," my voice is soft, the sheer panic I was feeling earlier was washed away by Mack's embrace. "Can I talk to you for a sec?"

Chris nods at me and I cross the floor, sitting lightly on the edge of his bed.

"Mom, I'm sorry I snuck to the grave." Chris sits up and looks at me with eyes so sad I instantly choke up.

"I know you are honey. You really gave me a scare."

"Mom, do you think I'm bad? I mean, I know I've been doing a lot of bad stuff. Do you think it's too late to be good now?" He twists the edge of his comforter in his hands and looks down.

"You're not bad. You've just made some bad choices, Chris. Everyone does. Even I've made bad choices." *Like not telling Mack he's your father.* The thought flits through my mind leaving a fiery trail of guilt.

"You have?" Chris looks up at me, but still clutches the blanket in his hands. It reminds me of when he was three and he wouldn't give up his baby blanket. I finally had enough of trying to coax him to stop dragging it everywhere, so when he was sleeping one night I snuck it out of his room and cut it up, stuffing the evidence in the bottom of the trash can.

Chris looked high and low for that stupid blanket, eventually finding a strand of his favorite blue blankie covered in coffee grounds and dust at the edge of the can. He pulled out the shred of blanket and wrapped it around his little hands, refusing to let it go, like a little boxer taping his hands before a fight. And what a fight he put up! I finally gave in to him, letting him keep that frayed fabric in his room until he was ready to let it go.

"Yep, even I have. You can't get through life without making mistakes. It's how we learn. It doesn't make you bad, it makes you human."

His chin quivers and his eyebrows drop as tears slide down the edge of his nose. "So, you still love me then? You're not mad at me?" he whispers.

I lean in and wrap my arms around him, "Of course I love you! Nothing can change that, honey. Not a single thing. We're gonna have good times and bad, but I'm always going to love you, Christopher! A mother never stops loving her kids, so I'm sorry, but you're just stuck with me loving you forever and ever and ever!" I squeeze him tight.

"Ok, Mom! You can let go now," my son's voice is muffled by my bear hug and I smile. "Oh, all right. I guess it's not cool to hug your Mom anymore, huh?" I tease him.

"No, I'm growing up you know. Mack said that I'm the man of the house." He puffs his chest out proudly.

"I know he did, but don't be in too big of a rush to grow up, ok? And don't think that you're too big to talk to me when things are getting hard for you. We've got to stick together, you and I. Got it?"

"Got it," Chris smiles and slides back down against his pillow. His eyelids look like they weigh a hundred pounds, but he's still fighting to keep them open.

I give his hand a squeeze and walk over to his door. "Goodnight Chris. Have sweet dreams, honey."

"I will." he mumbles back. "Oh, and Mom?"

"Yeah, hon?" I turn and look at him snuggled up in his bed. There's the boy I forgot I had. Looking so innocent and being so sweet.

"If you want to marry Mack, I just want you to know that it's ok with me." He smiles and closes his eyes, resting his head.

I don't even know what to say to that, and from the soft snores coming from Chris, I don't think I need to say anything.

"Good night Chris." I turn off his light and close the door, leaning my head back against it, I think about what he just said.

Kids are so perceptive! It's amazing what they see, what they know. Us adults could learn a thing or two from them.

CHAPTER 25:

Year - 2014

Mack

I hear Lauren shuffling around upstairs, I imagine she's probably getting me a blanket to crash on the couch with. It's been a crazy night; I'm guessing she's exhausted after all the drama. I listen to her feet softly padding down the stairs. My mouth drops open when I see her bare legs through the bannister. My eyes travel up her body to the tiny booty shorts and fitted tank top she's wearing. Oh my God, she's a fucking tease!

"What are you wearing?" My voice is louder than I intended, I clear my throat and try to turn down the volume, "Are you trying to kill me?" I immediately stand up and walk over to her. Like she's gravity or a magnetic pull. Like science itself has created a new law that refuses to let me stay away from her.

"This?" She looks down over her tiny clothes, then up at me, batting her dark eyelashes innocently. "This is just what I wear to bed."

"If that's what you wear to bed, then I think I'm going to need to keep you company," I run my hands down her back and press my body against hers.

"No," she says quietly.

"What?" I heard her, but I'm hoping my ears are mistaken.

"No, you can't come to bed with me."

So much for not hearing her right.

"Because I want you right here. Right now." She presses her tits into me. She's not wearing a bra, her dark nipples are little diamonds under her flimsy top, begging me to suck on them. I slide my hand down her back and under the edge of her shorts, grabbing her fat cheek in my hand tight, I push her against my hardening cock.

"Listen to me, Lauren. You need to know that this is what you want, you understand? You're always going on about how you're not one of my fan-club bimbos or whatever, and you're right, you're not." I wrap my hand in her coarse hair and firmly kiss her, squeezing her beautiful ass until she squirms up against my cock.

Fuck she feels good. I can't wait to feel her tight pussy again. I can smell her desire and it takes more will power than I knew I had not to pull her little shorts down to her knees, whirl her around and fuck her against the wall.

I pull my lips away from hers and Lauren sighs, her eyes still closed. "What's wrong?" She flutters them open.

"Nothing is wrong. I just need to know, right now, if you're ready to move on with your life. Cause, when we fuck. Not if, when, I'm not interested in having you for a night. I can get that from any girl. Hell, I can get it from a group of them, at the same time if I want."

Fire flashes in her brown eyes and her lips turn downward. "I'm well aware of your reputation, Mack."

"Good, cause it's all true. I'm sure I've earned every word of it. Listen to me, I'm not telling you this to make you jealous," I smile, "even though it's awfully cute on you."

"I'm not jealous," she lies, looking to the side.

"Good, because I don't want those girls. I want you. Only you, you understand? I need you to be ready to move on because when I fuck you, I'm making you mine, Lauren. I won't ever just watch you leave my life again."

"I never left you the first time. You left me." She's still pouting. Her lips sticking out at me, it's so cute. I grab her chin and kiss her again and her pout melts like butter on my lips.

"You're right," I whisper, "and I won't be leaving you again either. So, do you still want me?" I slide my fingers between her ass cheeks and push them forward until they dip into her soft, wet pussy. She's dripping for me, there's no denying what she wants, and I'm only too happy to give it to her, if she'll agree.

"I do. I really do," she moans, pressing her mound down against my hand.

I pull my hand back out of her shorts and wrap both my hands around her thighs, gripping them tight and pulling them open around me, I lift her off the ground and guide her legs around my waist. I walk her back across the floor toward the couch. "Good, cause I'm gonna fuck you until you can't move anymore," I growl.

CHAPTER 26:

Year - 2014

Mack

I toss Lauren down onto the sofa and she gives a little squeal. She flops down and her head falls back against the cushion. I'm not waiting for a special invitation. Before she even has a chance to lift her head back up, I climb on top of her, straddling her legs between mine. I hold her brown hands in mine and pull her up toward me until she's sitting pinned underneath me.

Lauren looks up at me with the same excitement she had in her eyes when we were teenagers. I remember how she made me wait until she officially turned eighteen before she'd let me fuck her. I mean, every teenaged boy practically spends a third of their life jerking off, but with her making me wait, it probably went up to fifty percent of my time.

The first few times I had her, I didn't have a clue how to really make her cum. I was just a dumb kid, fumbling in the darkness of inexperience. Now my blindfold has been lifted and I'm gonna show her that all these bimbos she's been getting jealous of have served their purpose.

She'll be sending them thank you cards.

"I can't move," Lauren looks up at me coyly. The twinkle in her gorgeous brown eyes tells me she isn't complaining.

"Good, I've got you right where I want you." I gather the fabric of her shirt over the edge of my fingers and pull it up off her body as she lifts her hands over her head to make it easier for me.

Her big tits bounce slightly when she drops her arms back by her sides, like they're taunting me. Daring me to take her. I slide my hands under her sweet ass and release her from the leg lock I've been holding her in. I scoop her beautiful ass up off the couch and plop her down on my throbbing cock.

"Oh!"

I don't give her a chance to think or to speak. Just feel. Dropping my head, I lick her perfect, almond skin from her collar bone to her mahogany nipple. Closing my lips around it, she moans to the ceiling, throwing her head back. I softly pucker my lips around her little diamond tip and flicker my tongue, gently battering her nipple. I glance up at her and graze the sharp edge of my teeth against her.

"Ahh," she yelps, but she grinds her hot little pussy down against my hard cock, still confined by these stupid jeans. I've never hated anything as much as I hate these pants right now.

I immediately give her little pebble another soft swish of my tongue, kissing it better before I move my head over and start doing the same thing to her other perfect nipple.

Fuck she's sexy. I can't tell you the amount of women who've dressed up or brought friends to the party just to get me half as excited as Lauren wearing a simple pair of booty shorts.

Her hands slide down over my shoulders and I feel the sharp tips of her nails dig into my skin as she twists her hips on top of me. I don't expect the burst of pain as she scrapes her nails across my flesh until I can feel the little cuts she's leaving on my back.

"Hey!" I stop teasing her full tits and look up at her smirking face.

"What?" She bats her eyelashes like a doll, "two can play that game," her pink lips turn up into a sultry smile.

"Oh, is that so? We'll just see about that," I grab her hands and wrap my hand around both her wrists so she can't pull that little stunt again. Not unless I want her to.

Pulling her arms high above her head, I throw her down onto the couch under my control. I'll let her use them again, when I decide what I want her to do to me. Until then, she's gonna lie here and squirm under me until she can't take anymore.

"God, Mack, I want you. I've always wanted you. Please let me see you? Let me feel you inside me," she begs.

"You're not ready yet," I let my eyes feast on her shamelessly. Savoring every inch of her skin from her long neck to her perky tits. She's too sexy, and the crazy part is, she doesn't even know it. Not like I do. Most women who look half as good as Lauren are used to every guy chasing them down. They get an attitude that she doesn't have. She's the most stunning woman I've ever met, and she's still so down to earth. She defies logic and rules. There are no games with her, no laws. Hell, even lying on her back, her perky tits seem to defy the law of gravity, so maybe she is some kind of magic.

And she's mine.

My eyes' gaze is interrupted rudely by the fabric of her little shorts, covering her modestly.

I've got no fucking time for modesty.

"Keep your hands up," I growl, releasing her wrists from my grasp. Lauren bites her pouty bottom lip and nods in response. "Good girl," I love a woman who knows when to challenge me and when to let me have my way.

I drag my fingertips down her ribs and over her little belly, protruding a little in the way a woman's body does once she's carried a child. Perfectly curved. I dig my fingers under the hips of each side of her shorts and tug them down to her knees in one quick pull.

The little patience I've had is rewarded as I look down onto her glistening pussy. With just a short trim of hair covering her, and her sweet nectar ripe for savoring, she looks like the sweetest peach ready to be devoured.

I quickly look into Lauren's eyes and she watches me intently, her arms still perfectly still above her head. "But don't worry, I'm gonna make sure I get you ready."

I pull her little shorts down the rest of her legs and toss them over my shoulder onto the floor. Sliding down between her thick thighs, I pinch my fingers into the meat of her legs as I hold them open wide. Her pussy is totally exposed now, the dark brown of her petals contrasting against the soft pink of her sensitive nub.

I bury my face between her thighs and pull one of her dark lips into my mouth, tugging it softly as I let my tongue tease her sweet clit. She tastes like heaven. And I should know, I caught a glimpse of it in the desert. Funny how in the moment I was facing death, I saw her. She must be my eternal life.

I circle my wet tongue over her nub as she tries to twist her hips in anticipation. My hands have her pinned to the couch though, and as long as she doesn't move her arms, she's completely under my power.

Sliding my tongue down the length of her pussy, I spread her fat cheeks and dip my lips between them until I have my tongue pressed against her tight asshole.

Lauren gasps and she stiffens out under my hands. But she doesn't tell me to stop or say she doesn't like it. She just seems surprised. I flicker my tongue against her until she's squirming and bearing down against me. I slide back up to her sweet clit just to keep her on the edge.

I finally let go of her thigh and push my fingertip into her pussy, feeling her muscles contract around me, trying to milk me.

In good time, baby.

God, she's still so fucking tight! She hasn't changed since she was eighteen.

I know I can't wait much longer to make her mine. I need to feel her tight pussy around my cock. My lips close around her clit and I suckle it lightly as I flutter my tongue against her relentlessly. Lauren is gasping and breathing a string of incoherent words. The way her walls keep gripping down on my finger, I can tell she's very close.

"Mack! Oh, my God!" Her body tightens up under me, ever muscle contracting as she cums for me.

I pull my head away, knowing how sensitive she'll be after that, but keep thrusting my finger inside her as I watch her pant for air. Her hairline is covered in tiny droplets of sweat and she has the arms I told her not to move thrown over her eyes. I'll let it go this time. Clearly she needs a minute.

Lauren moves her arm and smiles down at me bashfully. Her hips keep climbing to meet my finger rhythmically fucking her pussy.

"I think you're ready now."

"That was amazing."

"That was nothing." I reluctantly stop fingering her little box and sit up enough to pull off my shirt. I stand up to get the pants off. With my prosthetic leg, I need to be careful about how I pull down my jeans. It's probably not the most graceful way to undress, but it'll get the job done. Finally, I pull off my underwear and smile down to Lauren as she licks her lips hungrily for me.

"Wanna taste, baby?" I stroke my rock hard cock and watch her eyes widen as they travel down every inch of my member.

"I do." she purrs.

I hold my dick at the base and hover the tip over her lips. Lauren quickly swipes her tongue over the tip, licking off the tiny bead of precum and then opens her mouth wide as she takes my thick cock deep into her mouth. I let my hand rest on the back of her head, guiding her slowly down my shaft until I can hear her throat protest with a slight gagging.

"Sorry, I won't go that deep. Not in your mouth anyway," I reassure her as her eyes water a bit and look up at me.

"Mmmm," I'm not sure if she's agreeing or arguing, but either way, it feels fucking amazing.

"Yeah, baby, just like that." I let go of her head and just watch as Lauren slides her lips up and down the length of my shaft. I can feel the tension in my balls building as I get swept away by the sensation of her wet tongue sweeping over the tip of my cock.

Fuck. If she doesn't stop soon, I'm going to cum down her throat.

"You need to stop," I whisper unconvincingly. Lauren either doesn't hear me or doesn't listen. My balls tighten up and I'm gonna blow my load if I don't pull out. I manage to take a step back, releasing myself from her perfect pout.

I know I'm already a decorated veteran, but I want another damned medal for the self control that took. Hell, I want a chest full of medals!

"I can finish you and we can have sex later," she looks up at me, almost pleading. I've gotta admit, it's tempting as fuck.

"No," my voice is hoarse. It's amazing I can talk at all, really. "I've been missing you for ten years, I don't want to wait one more second for you. I want you right now."

I kneel down between her legs and she opens them wide for me. I'm not the only one who doesn't want to wait anymore.

I grab my cock and slide it up and down just allowing the tip to tease her clit as I get myself back under control.

Fuck control.

I press the head of my cock into her wet pussy and wrap my other hand around the back of her neck, pressing all of my weight into her. She breathes in sharp as I bury my cock into her pussy. She's so tight, I'm almost questioning if I ever took her virginity the first time around.

"Oh!" Lauren's eyes are wide and she squirms a little under me. I've been told I can be a bit much to take in one stroke, but I can't help myself with her. I know I should pull back, let her adjust to my girth and go slow, but I can't.

I thrust my cock deep into her until my balls smack up against her plump ass cheeks. Still holding her head in a vice grip, I finally pull back a little bit and then fuck her hard. I let myself get lost in her, let my cock bury inside her over and over as she whimpers in my ear.

I don't know how I've ever wasted time with any other girl. How I've ever let so much time go by. How I ever walked away. She's amazing. I've fucked more women than I can keep track of, and I know not a single one has felt like her. Like she was actually made to fit my body and mine alone.

My breathing is getting heavy and so are my balls as I just keep fucking Lauren like I just got out of prison. In a way I have. Even if it was a prison of my own making.

"Oh, Mack, I'm gonna …" Her pussy squeezes around me and I arch my back so I can look down the length of our bodies. I want to see what's mine milking my thick cock for every drop of cum I'm about to give her. Lauren drives her nails back into my back in the same spot she carved out before. The sharp pain and the sensation of her tight pussy quivering around me is too much. A wave of pleasure floods through me as I fill her with spurts of my seed.

I feel light headed as I collapse against Lauren on the couch. Her legs are tangled around me in a full body hug and my cock is still twitching inside her.

Cold realization washes over me as it occurs to me that I didn't ask about protection. People have been calling me Captain America since I came back to US soil, but they could just as easily have been calling me Captain Condom.

"Damn it," I hiss and pull out of Lauren. Her eyes cloud over as confusion washes her face.

"What? You have regrets?" The pain is all over her words. Regrets? How could she think that?

"No, I just should've used protection. I got caught up." I chide myself.

"Why? I mean, you're ok, aren't you?" Panic tinges her words as she searches for meaning in mine.

"No, no. I mean, yes. I don't have anything. It's not that." I kiss the tip of her nose.

"Oh," I can see the tension melt away from her shoulders as she lies her head back against the arm of the couch. "Well, don't worry about it then. I'm on birth control still. I don't know why I didn't stop when Joel passed. I guess it was just a habit." She shrugs looking down to the cushions beneath us.

"Yeah, but birth control doesn't work that great for us, does it?" Lauren doesn't blink. She keeps staring at the cushion like she's memorizing it.

"What do you mean?" she whispers to the couch.

"I mean Chris. He's mine isn't he?" I finally ask the question that I've been wondering since I looked at the pictures. "He is my son, isn't he Lauren?" I look down at her and if it wasn't for the pulse wildly beating in her neck, I would think she was dead. She doesn't move. Doesn't blink. I don't think she's even breathing. "Lauren?" I don't mean to raise my voice, but it comes out sharper than I intend.

She snaps her head up and looks me straight in the eyes. Her brown eyes seem darker, more somber.

"Yes."

CHAPTER 27:

Year - 2014

Lauren

Scooting back on the couch, I pull my knees into my chest and fold my arms around my legs. I suddenly feel so exposed. So vulnerable. And it has nothing to do with being naked.

Mack knows that he has a son. This secret I've been carrying for ten years has finally been lifted from my soul. I thought when this day came I would feel lighter, not sick.

"Yes, he's yours." I answer him again. Resting my head on my knees, I look up at him from under my eyelashes. I'm not sure how he's going to react. What he's going to say. I watch storm clouds roll in over his face as he battles the emotions he'll never share with me. Mack was never one to talk about his feelings, even before the military. Now even less so.

"Why didn't you tell me? Why didn't you get a hold of me at West Point?" He shakes his head slowly; his voice is monotone. I can't tell if he thinks this is good news or the worst thing he's heard. His furrowed brows aren't really giving me a lot of information.

"I thought about it. Trust me. You have no idea how many nights I fought with myself. It was hard. Please don't think I made the decision lightly. I didn't. For the first three years of Chris's life, I was a single mother. I second guessed not telling you every single day. Especially when I was getting my degree and trying to look after my baby."

"Then why didn't you?" Mack stands up and runs his hand over the back of his head. He walks over to the photos I caught him looking at earlier and stares down at them, his hand still resting on his neck as he looks back over the photos. My eyes sweep down his naked body, I wish he wouldn't put distance between us. I wish he'd hold me close and talk to me about this.

"Instead you let another man raise my child as his own? I mean, does that seem right to you? Did I hurt you that badly, Lauren? Was I so terrible to you that you didn't even let me know I had a son in this world?" The muscles in his back flex tight.

"No, you weren't bad to me. You did hurt me, yes." I admit, fresh tears sting my eyes as if the wound of him choosing his country over me happened yesterday. I guess it's more like a burn than a wound. A burn that looks alright on the surface but keeps destroying the layers of skin underneath. A burn that radiates pain deep inside, long after it should have healed.

"So you got back at me by keeping Chris from me?" his voice wavers, he still won't face me. I hate talking to the back of his head, but I understand if he can't look at me right now. I hug my knees tighter to my body, desperate to feel Mack's arms around me. I wonder if I ever will again.

"No, it had nothing to do with that!" I can't believe he'd accuse me of keeping Chris out of his life because I had hurt feelings. What does he think of me? "Yes, I was hurt. Yes, I was angry. But I never kept it from you because of how you decided to leave. Let me remind you, it was you who decided to walk away and leave me here while you went off to pursue your dreams, Mack." My tone has a razor's edge.

"Lauren, I was doing what I thought was right. You remember how Ben died. What was I supposed to do, forget about the one thing that I cared about and stay here just because you didn't like my decision?" He finally turns to face me and I wish he'd turn back around. His eyes flash with anger, but under the anger I can see the betrayal he's feeling tossing around on the ocean blue storm of his eyes.

"I thought I was the one thing you cared about," I whisper, I feel like I swallowed a rock.

"You know what I mean," he snaps.

"No, I don't. And I certainly didn't then. Do you remember what you told me on prom night? How it was the perfect time for you to get into West Point because you had to be a certain age and couldn't be married and …"

"I couldn't have kids," he finishes my sentence. The anger fades from his eyes as he stares down at the floor.

"Exactly. I didn't keep Chris from you because you left me for West Point. It wasn't some kind of revenge, Mack. I kept him from you because I knew how much West Point meant to you. I knew you would come back and look after us, but that you'd always be full of regret. You'd never get the chance to go again. Ever. I didn't want us to be a weight around your neck." I confess.

"You shouldn't have made that decision for me," his voice is flat. Defeated. My heart squeezes in my chest thinking that I did this to him.

"You're right. I was young and stupid. I never should have let you go, either. I should've tried to make it work when you said you wanted to do the long distance thing. I admit I wasn't a genius at eighteen."

"And what about in your twenties? What about after I graduated? You still never looked me up?" He meets my eyes and I see a flash of lightening on the stormy seas of his crystal blues.

"You're right. I met Joel in college and we ended up married. I guess after that I didn't think about contacting you as much. I figured it would just make everything even more complicated. You never came back to Colorado, so I never knew if you got married or had other kids or anything. I guess I just thought it was better to let sleeping dogs lie." I leave out how I still agonized about it for years. How many nights I searched for him on Facebook. How many times I tried to find his e-mail address.

"This is so fucked up, Lauren. I mean, how did any of this happen anyway? Didn't you tell me you were on the pill then too?" Mack paces back and forth in front of my couch. I hold my hand out to him and he looks down at it like I'm holding up a foreign food.

"Please, Mack, sit down with me." I plead.

He looks at me and grasps my hand. My heart flutters like a hummingbird's wings with hope.

"Ok." He settles back onto the couch and looks over at me. I can see the suspicion coursing through his veins, but at least he's giving me the chance to talk.

"Thank you," I breathe deep, feeling like I'm taking in the first breath after a deep dive. "You're right, I was on the pill. I mean, you remember how diligent I was with it. I had a timer on my cellphone and everything."

"I remember." His jaw is tight.

"I don't know if you remember that about a week before prom I got an ear infection?" I look into his eyes but I don't see a flash of recognition. "Anyway, the doctor gave me a string of antibiotics and I didn't realize back then that it makes your birth control not work that great. At least it did for me. So, yeah, Chris happened. Not that I would trade him for the world." My mother's guilt sweeps over me; all this talk about our son like he's a mistake isn't sitting well on my heart.

"Fuck, that's a lot to take in." Mack looks down at his palms like he's trying to read them. If I trace his love line, will I be there? Or is my place always going to be in his past?

"I know. Just so you know, when Joel passed, I did start looking you up again to tell you. I was tracking down old high school friends to see if they knew what happened to you. Then I was watching the eleven o'clock news one night and I saw the footage of you over there. It was crazy. I'd been trying so hard to track you down and then, there you were on my television." I remember how I sobbed uncontrollably as I watched Mack covered in blood. The news had pixelated the lower half of his leg missing, but it was clear as day what had happened to him.

"Shit. You saw that, huh?" He looks over at me and moves closer to me, gently placing his large hand on my foot.

"Everyone in America saw that, Mack. The president saw it. So, yeah, I saw it too. It just felt like, since I knew what you were going to be up against with rehab and everything, like it was a sign to leave it alone. You were going to have enough on your plate, you know? It didn't feel like a good time to fire off an e-mail about Chris, that's for damned sure." I place my hand on top of his and the warmth of his skin soothes me.

"I can see that. That makes sense." He looks over at me, into me. "Does he know?"

"That you're his father? No. He doesn't. Chris knows that Joel wasn't his biological Dad, and that he was adopted. I mean the kid is smart, he figured it out the same way you did." I sweep my hand out toward the photographs. "I've never told him who his real father is though."

Silence grows between us and fills the air like a scream. A scream would be better actually. My skin begins to prickle as I wait for Mack to say something. Anything. Does he hate me? Does he want to be in our lives?

"I'm sorry," Mack's voice cuts through my thoughts.

"What? Why are you sorry?"

"I'm sorry that I never looked back. I was young too, I was hurt that you wouldn't even try to stay together when I left, so I tried to erase you from my memory. I didn't realize that it was impossible, you were more than a memory. You were etched on my soul. When I lost my leg, and ... my men ..." his voice wavers as his emotions battle on his face. He clears his throat and his eyes focus back on mine, "You were there."

"You mean you thought of me?" I try to make sense of his words.

"No, you were there. I could see you. Smell you. Taste you. I felt your hand on mine. I knew that if I died then, it would be with a heart full of regret for ever letting you leave. I knew I could never die happy until I found you again."

Tears prick the corners of my eyes and the rock in my throat feels even heavier as I struggle not to cry. "I never thought I'd see you again," I confess. "I already felt like a piece of me had died the day you went to West Point."

He scoots over on the couch and puts his arm around me, I lie my head against his chest and let his heartbeat sing me a lullaby. "Were back together now," he soothes me, running his hand over my hair. "All three of us. We're gonna make this work. Ok?" He grabs my shoulders and holds me inches from his face. I'm lost in his eyes, transfixed by them.

"Yes."

CHAPTER 28:

Year - 2014

Mack

"Hey, sexy." I sneak up behind Lauren and wrap my arms around her, pulling her plump ass back against my cock.

I watched her come into the building this morning, her hair perfectly in place and her uniform trim and pressed. Miles away from the naked wild cat I was gagging with my cock only hours before.

"Mack, you can't sneak up on me like this," she pushes my hands down from her hips and twists around. Her lips are pressed into a solid line and she's got her cute little nose scrunched up at me.

"Aww, c'mon, you don't want to have a quickie in the supply closet? Where's that naughty girl I was flipping around all weekend, huh?" I pull her tight against me and I can see her pulse quicken in her neck. I let my hands slide down over her perfect ass and cup it, pulling her against my stiffening cock. Maybe she just needs a little inspiration.

Lauren quickly looks over my shoulder toward the closet door, she doesn't need to worry though, I closed it behind me.

"A quickie? Are you crazy? This is where I work, Mack. It's bad enough that you spent the weekend at my house," she presses her hands firmly against my chest and steps back, "you're gonna get me fired."

"I didn't spend the weekend at your house, I was visiting my wonderful Aunt Mildred, remember?" I smirk, but she isn't budging. Neither is the fixed line she has her lips in.

"No, I can't," she hisses.

I want to sweep my hand over the medical crap crowding one of these metal tables and flip her around, bending her over it. I want to hold her down with one hand and rip her pants down with the other, fucking her wildly until she's dripping with my cum. The idea makes my cock throb painfully and I adjust myself so the sensitive skin isn't pressing directly against my zipper.

I may want to do that, but I won't. I'm a persistent guy, but I know what lines can't be crossed.

"Fine," I hold my hands up in surrender. "I just thought you looked really sexy this morning and wanted to show you how crazy you're making me. I get it though, no quickies at work." I step back, giving her some space.

Lauren looks back over my shoulder at the door nervously. "No anything at work, Mack. I can't lose this job, especially not for messing around with a patient. I'll never find another hospital that will hire me after that. Look," she closes the distance between us and runs the back of her fingers down my cheek and over my beard, "I want you, ok. Trust me, you have no idea," the glint in her eyes speaks volumes. "We'll figure this out, I promise. Now, please, get out of here before someone else needs something out of here." She urges, but she doesn't break away from me. Lauren stands her ground, her breasts lightly pressing up against my chest.

I hold her chin between my thumb and forefinger and blanket her lips with mine, a hard kiss for how hard she's made me. Lauren relaxes against me and her mouth opens, inviting me to take the kiss deeper. As our tongues collide, I slowly step her back, one step at a time, until her back is flat against the wall. I pin her in place with my hips and grind my ready cock against her hot little pussy as our kiss continues. Like I said, I'm persistent.

A stream of light floods in from the door and I pull back quickly. Lauren gasps and runs the palms of her hands down over her shirt like she's trying to iron them to her body.

"Uh, Doctor Galt. Um, Mack, I mean, um, Captain Forrester

just needed …" her eyes search the closet frantically as I turn to face the cock-block at the door.

"I needed some bandages," I state matter-of-factly. My eyes leveling him.

"That's not what it looked like from here," cherry stains his face and he blows his cheeks out like a puffer fish. "This is highly unprofessional," his face twitches with irritation as he looks over at Lauren. I don't need to look at her to know what she looks like right now. I don't want to see the shame tattooed to her face.

"What's highly unprofessional about my nurse getting me bandages?" I interrupt his glare. "If you ask me, that's kinda the definition of professionalism right there."

His eyes flicker wildly as he attempts to push his chest out. These small guys are always the same, like little Chihuahuas trying to be pit bulls. "I don't want to hear it, Captain. I know what I saw." He looks back over at Lauren, who's still silently being shielded by my body. "And if you think for one second that this isn't going to be reprimanded, then you are mistaken. I've never seen such amoral conduct in a hospital. This man is your patient, Nurse Brickman. This little … relationship," he spits out the word like it burned the roof of his mouth, "is against your medical oath and it's against the law."

I can see him winding up like one of those symbol crashing monkey dolls we used to play with as kids. Nope. Not happening. Fire burns up in my gut, licking flames of fury into my throat.

Who the fuck does this guy think he is? He doesn't get to talk to my woman like that! My hands ball up at my sides and my eyes narrow into slits.

"No, you listen, doc. I've told you that Nurse Brickman has been professional, which is much more than I can say about you right now. And the last time I checked, I walked in here with a media team and worldwide news coverage when I came to your little hospital. So, if you want to pursue this, who do you think people are going to fucking believe? A national war hero who left his leg in the desert for his country? Or you?" I sneer down at him.

Galt's chest deflates and his shoulders drop as he considers my words. "Listen, I'm not trying to start anything like that," he starts back pedalling. "The media doesn't need to be involved in this. I'm just trying to run a hospital here. It's important that our staff follow proper procedures and conduct themselves appropriately." His eyes flash at Lauren.

"I know, I'm sorry," she finally finds her voice behind me and the words scrape across my eardrums like the squeal of Styrofoam being twisted.

"No, you didn't do anything wrong. Don't say sorry." I put my hand in the air, interrupting whatever incriminating thing she's about to confess.

"As for me being a patient, I can leave this hospital at any time. In fact, I'll be checking out today, thank you. I don't need this attitude or negativity from a place that's supposed to be helping me heal." Galt's mouth puckers tight like an asshole. With the shit he's been spewing, I think it's appropriate.

"I'll be doing some more media appearances soon with my blade, too," I continue. "They can really go one of two ways. I can sing the praises of your fantastic rehabilitation center and shine a light on the wonderful care I've received here," I look back at Lauren, I hate the fear I can see in her eyes. "Or, if you want to pursue reprimanding Nurse Brickman here, I can shine an entirely different spotlight on your center. It's up to you."

I stroll across the floor and Galt's mouth is gaping wide. If his lips looked was an asshole a couple seconds ago, then it just got fucked.

"Captain, I don't see that there's any reason you need to cut your rehabilitation short. I'm sure we can discuss this like civilized adults," he pleads but doesn't try to block the door as I approach.

"I've done all the talking I intend to do; the rest is up to you." I stare straight into his little eyes and walk out the closet door.

"Captain Forrester, please, wait!" he calls but I continue on down the hall, leaving Lauren and her career dangling by a thread behind me.

Shit. How am I going to make up for this one?

CHAPTER 29:

Year – 2014

Lauren

This has been the longest day I've ever had. I've been riding a roller coaster of emotions for hours and it's making me nauseous. It feels like this morning, in the supply closet with Mack, was weeks ago.

I'm starting to feel numb now. I've gone from dripping wet with desire to paralyzed with fear to utter disbelief as I watched Mack make good on his word and pack up his bags.

By the time he walked out the door, Dr. Galt was practically begging him to stay. Only Mack could get caught breaking rules and have people apologize to him for inconveniencing him with them in the first place.

That was about four hours ago. Ever since I've been trying to lay low and look busy, but I can't stop agonizing over what Mack is doing. He hasn't been answering my texts or calls. I have no idea where he went, or where he plans to stay.

It's such a mess.

In twenty minutes I'll be off for the night and hopefully we can figure it out together. A light tap on my shoulder makes me jump from my thoughts.

"I need to talk to you in my office, Ms. Taylor," my chief gives me a scalding glance and jerks his head as he hands out his orders.

Damn it.

"Uh, sure," I follow him as he marches down the corridor. My stomach feels like I ate lead for lunch. I'm so fired. There's no way I'm not getting fired. Now what am I going to do? How am I going to look after Chris? Pay the mortgage? My thoughts spin around in a cyclone of panic as I approach Dr. Galt's office.

He opens the door and storms into the room reserved for the chief of medical staff. I scurry in behind him.

"Sit down there, please," he points to the chair in front of his imposing desk and doesn't wait for me to respond before sitting down on the other side.

His desk looks comically large for him, is he sitting on a couple of phone books back there? I fight the smile trying to take over my lips, but he looks like a cartoon.

Be serious, I scold myself silently. What is going on with you? Maybe my mother was right all those years ago, when I was eleven and got caught dropping balloons full of ketchup on cars from the overpass with Mack. She said then that he was a bad influence on me. There's just something about him that makes me relax and stop trying to make everything perfect. Something that makes being bad feel so damned good.

"You know I can't let you leave for the day without addressing some issues." Galt looks across his desk at me, snapping me back into the present.

"Yes, I understand." My heart picks up the pace, pumping like a little drummer boy.

"I don't think I need to explain to you the awkward position you've put me in here," he rubs his thumb and forefinger over his wedding ring. For a second, I try to imagine the woman who decided that this man was the one for her. All I can picture are arranged marriages, mail-order brides and robot sex dolls. My money is on the sex doll.

"As you can imagine, it's important that we maintain our reputation as a world class rehabilitation center," he continues. Waves of guilt begin to wash up over me. "People come from all around the globe to receive care here, they do that because we're known for our cutting edge clinics, but also because we're known for our highly professional, top of the line staff." My boss rolls his ring around his finger and the guilt rises like a tide.

"I know that, sir. And I don't believe that what happened today needs to change any of that." I hope I can plead my case.

"You don't? How do you expect our facility to remain internationally respected when," he clears his throat and every muscle in my body tightens? Here it comes. The pink slip and a walk to the front door. Tears spring to the corners of my eyes and I try to think of what I can possibly say to save my job. "When one of the biggest war heroes that America has ever known decides to cut his rehabilitation here early?"

Huh?

"I, um, I'm not sure?" I blink in surprise. My mind is trying to sift through his words like a gold panner in the Klondike, searching for a tiny glint of something familiar.

"It doesn't look good at all." He looks up at me with his eyebrows climbing skyward, worry clouds his eyes.

"I don't think anyone would really notice that Mack, er, that Captain Forrester isn't a patient here anymore." I try to reassure him. "It's not like they knew his program here or had a timeline of how long he was expected to stay."

"Yes they did, I gave them one when we had the media conference," he answers glumly.

Of course he did.

"Ok, but still, people discharge early for all kinds of reasons all of the time. I really don't think you have anything to worry about." I reassure him.

Galt's eyebrows settle back down and the corners of his mouth twinge, almost imperceptibly. I can't be sure, but I think he's happy. "That's true, as long as he doesn't bad mouth our facility during his upcoming interviews." His mouth turns back down. It was fun while it lasted.

"He won't. I've known Mack since I was a child. He was just blowing smoke. He won't say anything that will damage the hospital." My mom heart twinges for him and I almost want to reach across his overcompensating desk and hold his hand.

Almost. I mean, let's not get crazy here.

Galt nods slowly, digesting my words. "He said the same thing when I called him earlier," he confides.

Wait just one hot second, Mack answered his calls but couldn't return a single text from me?

"He did make a request that you be awarded a few days off to give you time to deal with personal issues you've been having. It's no problem, of course, especially since your sole patient left today and also left a hole in your schedule."

"I'm sorry, you were talking to Mack? And he told you what, exactly?" I drop the "Captain Forrester" routine and cut to the chase. I think it's safe to say that the cat is out of the bag anyway.

"He mentioned the troubles you've been having with your son, and now with this adjustment you'll need to make to your program,

I don't see a problem with you having a few days leave. I just wish you would've let me know that you were having issues. That's what I'm here for." He catches my eye quickly, but I can't see any sincerity in him.

"Well, that's very kind of you," I answer through clenched teeth. Who the fuck does Mack think he is? First he follows me into the medical closet and almost gets me fired, then he tries to fix it by spilling secrets about my family? I'm fucking unimpressed. "However, I won't be needing any time off. I have everything under control, I can assure you." I hiss out my words.

"No need to thank me," Dr. Galt steamrolls over me. Did he actually listen to anything I just said? "I'm hoping that on your extra days off that I'm granting, you'll be able to speak with Captain Forrester and remind him of how well he was treated here? Just in case he has any hard feelings from our little outburst this morning." He doesn't wait for me to answer. Instead, he rolls his chair back and pulls out a drawer on his desk, clearly searching for something.

"I can assure you that I'll definitely be speaking to Captain Forrester." I nod. I won't tell him that I will most certainly be giving Mack a piece of my mind, but that I have no intention of being a walking infomercial for Spalding.

"That would be appreciated," he reaches into his drawer and shuffles around, pulling out a pink piece of construction paper. "Here, do you mind giving this to him? It's from my daughter. I was supposed to give it to him the day he arrived, but I must have forgotten." He slides the homemade card across the desk to my fingertips.

I pick it up and look at the sprawling message written by a child's hand. It has a picture of what I assume is Mack on the front with hearts around him. Inside she wrote, "Thank u. My hero!" My hand trembles a little as my throat feels like it's closing down. I struggle to dam up the flood of tears threatening to fall.

I'm not sure what's sadder, the fact that my boss didn't care enough about the card his daughter made to do anything but stuff it in a drawer, or the fact that he's only now trying to have it delivered so he can try to manipulate Mack into caring about this stupid hospital. My heart breaks for a little girl I've never met.

"Sure, I'll pass it along," I mumble, never taking my eyes off the card.

"Fantastic, ok, well enjoy your days off!" He dismisses me and I stand up, making my way to the door. "And, Ms. Brickman?"

"Yes?" I turn and look back at him.

"Just remember how very differently this meeting could have gone today when you're talking to him. Ok?" His eyes narrow and my skin prickles with rage.

"I will." I answer simply and walk out into the hall.

What a fucking douche.

CHAPTER 30:

Year - 2014

Lauren

I know I should head straight to mom's and pick up Chris. However, I turn up my street instead. I just need some down time to figure everything out. Nothing crazy. Just, like, an hour to get my head on straight about everything that's happened today. I slow to a crawl as I drive up to my house. Chelsea's silver SUV is parked in my driveway.

So much for that idea.

I could just keep driving. I could go until the car runs out of gas, or my heart runs out of rage, or I finally figure this mess out.

I pull in at my house and throw the car in park. Running away never solves anything. I've learned that the hard way. Reaching over to the passenger seat, I grab my purse and look at the pink paper card I tossed on there when I left Spalding. There's no real point in giving it to Mack, he'll see through Galt's pathetic attempts at manipulation a mile away.

I sigh as my eyes travel over the drawing on the front. The effort and detail her young hands put into drawing each shaky heart. No, screw that. I will give it to him. Not because I care about my boss and his games, but because someone needs to care about the little girl who worked so hard to make this for Mack.

Grabbing the card, I head into the house to see why Chelsea's here. If it isn't one thing, it's another.

"She's here! She's here!" My son's cries can be heard through my living room window as I walk by it.

Stepping inside, I can see Chris hopping around with excitement. Chelsea is on the couch sipping a coffee. If she only knew what Mack and I were doing on that couch last night, she wouldn't be sitting there. She'd probably go shower in some Lysol.

"Hey, what's going on?" I look at my sister.

"We're going to Elitch Gardens! And a hotel! It's gonna be awesome!" Chris practically vibrates in his skin.

"What?" I raise my eyebrows at Chelsea, but she just sips her coffee in response. Her eyes are twinkling at me. She's up to something.

"Good afternoon, beautiful." Mack struts in from the kitchen holding a mug that says "Supermom" on it. He's not the only one who gets to have a comic book alias. Although, I don't think kids will be saving up their allowance to buy the latest supermom editions any time soon.

What is he doing here? Just walking around my house like he's been there all his life. He holds out the mug to me. "Here you go, with a dash of milk. Just like you like it." His signature smirk is pasted to his face.

"Aww, isn't that sweet?" Chelsea chimes in. "Lauren, why don't you pour that in a travel mug so we can get this show on the road. I don't want to get stuck in rush hour traffic." My big sister bosses me around in her signature style.

"Where are you driving? What's going on?" I wrap my fingers around the warmth of the mug, ignoring Mack for the time being.

"Elitch Gardens! We're gonna go on all the rides, and sleep in a hotel, and get room service too! Right Mack?" Chris jumps around like a kid on Christmas morning. If that kid was on meth.

"Whoa? What?" My eyes flicker from my hyper child to his hot-headed father. "Mack, can I talk to you for a sec?" I put the coffee down on my mantle and walk through the kitchen and out the sliding door into the backyard. I don't check to see if he's following. I know he's not stupid enough to stay behind.

"Aww! Why are they talking?" Chris whines inside.

"Just give them a minute, honey." My sister consoles him as Mack slides the door shut behind us.

Suddenly, his arms slide around me and he hugs me from behind. "I wanted to surprise you with a little treat." He murmurs in my ear and I instinctively rest my head back against his chest. "I know today was pretty stressful for you, so I booked us a couple rooms at the Four Seasons and got us some passes at Elitch. I figure a little R & R will be good for you. Chelsea is going to share a room with Chris, so I'm going to have two days in a hotel with you to do whatever I want." His voice grows thick with desire.

I flutter my eyes closed for a moment and feel the tension ease from my shoulders. Dr. Galt's stupid face pops into my head and my tendons practically snap as the stress winds me back up. "Mack, you can't just spring things like this on me and call my boss and demand he give me days off." I pull away from him and turn to face him. "Today was ridiculous, I could've gotten fired you know. And you taking off and not answering my texts or calls was a pretty shitty thing to do to me. What were you thinking?"

"I wasn't thinking, I was reacting. I wasn't going to let that asshole threaten your job because of me. I know I didn't handle it the best."

"Didn't handle it the best? Mack you can't just do whatever pops into your mind. We're adults now, you have to act like one sometimes. I'm not sure what's going on with you. And then you just make plans with Chris and Chelsea without even talking to me? How did you think that was gonna go over?" My teeth are clenched together so tight that my jaw hurts.

Mack stands straighter as he squares off his shoulders and looks into my eyes. "I know today was a shit show, Lauren. I fucked up."

I can feel the anger begin to drain from my body along with my energy. "Look, I don't want to fight with you. The truth is, I'm worried about you. Chris told me about what happened at the grave the other night," I lower my voice and touch his hand gently.

Anger flashes in his eyes. Mack pulls his hand away. "I'm fine." he answers tersely.

"Are you sure? Cause you know it would be understandable if you needed a little help. You've been through a lot. More than any of us can imagine. Chris has only been going to his group therapy sessions twice now and look how much it's helped him. Maybe you can find a group ..."

"I said I'm fine." He juts out his chin and clenches his fists at his side. I can see him struggling with his demons and his temper. I'm not sure if he can win this battle though. Mack takes a deep breath and closes his eyes. When he opens them, the rage has passed and sorrow has crept into it's place.

"I know that I haven't always dealt with everything the best, ok? But I'm fine. Just let me deal with things the best way for me. Anyway, I wanted to say sorry for the way things happened today. That's why I wanted to make it right and treat you guys to a few days of fun. I thought it would be nice to spend time together as a family." His crystal blue eyes scan my face as my anger and my forgiveness battle it out.

"A family?" I mumble, his eyes holding me in place.

"Yeah, you, me, Chris. Our family. I asked Chelsea to come because I don't have a car and still need to learn to drive with my leg," he looks down at his prosthetic wearily. "And she agreed to come along and help look after Chris. Now we can start making up for some lost time together. We don't have to hide our relationship anymore, since I left Spalding. It's all good."

My mind keeps dancing around the word "family". It's something I've always dreamt of, sharing my life with Mack.

"What's in your hand?" He reaches over gently plucking the card from my fingers.

"It's a card. The chief's daughter made it for you." I don't bother telling him why he gave it to me. It doesn't matter.

A smile creeps across Mack's face as he looks down at the pink paper. "That's nice," he looks up at me, "I can't wait to get cute little homemade cards from our daughter."

"Our daughter?" My breath hitches in my throat. Mack steps toward me and wraps his arms around me.

"Of course. We make beautiful children. It'd be a damned shame to stop with one." His voice rumbles in my ear and I can feel my resistance melting away. "Why don't we go to Elitch? Let me make today up to you? I'd like to take Chris somewhere fun and then, once it's just you and me in the hotel room, I can really make things right." His eyes twinkle.

"Well," I press up against him, "I guess I do have the time off now."

"You do."

"And Chris is pretty excited to go."

"He is."

"So, I guess we can do that." I agree.

Mack kisses me and I melt into his arms. I love how the same man that can drag so much chaos into my life can also make me feel so protected from it. How does he do that?

I pull away and look back into his eyes, "But Mack?"

"Yes."

"You have to promise that you won't have anymore outbursts or anything else for that matter. Ok? I don't want Chris seeing you get like that; it's too upsetting for him."

"Cross my heart," he smiles and crosses a x over his chest.

I can't help but laugh. Mack will never really grow up, but that's what makes him so much fun to be around. A few days together as a family will be nice. Family. That word just fits so well. We're finally all together again.

As a family.

CHAPTER 31:

Year - 2014

Mack

"Mom! Did you see us? It was crazy!" Chris bounds up to Lauren excitedly.

"Way to go, little man! That roller coaster is crazy! I would've died if I went on that." Chelsea holds up her hand to Chris and he high fives it.

"I did see you, was it fun?" Lauren looks down at him with a smile.

"It was amazing! Can I go again? I just need to go pee first, but you can hold my place in the line and then when I get back you can go on it with me this time," he instructs Lauren. You gotta respect a man with a plan.

"No, hun. I'm with Chelsea on this, I would never go on a ride that fast. We're not all like Captain America over there," she winks at me. "The Ferris wheel is about as daring as I get."

"That's right, not everyone can be a hero," I tease her.

"Yeah, yeah. I think you've played that card already," she shoots back at me, busting my chops. God, I love her. "Besides," she looks back down at Chris, "your aunt and I are getting hungry. Don't you guys want to eat?"

"Yeah!" Chris jumps, instantly forgetting how much he wanted to get on the Brain Drain again.

"I'll tell ya what, bud," Chelsea looks down at him, "how about you go with your mom and find a bathroom. I'll head out with Mack to get us some pizza slices. That way we'll cut our time standing in line down. Ok?"

Lauren looks over at her sister with question marks in her eyes. "Doesn't it make more sense for you and I to get the food and for Mack to take Chris?"

"Nah," Chelsea waves her off casually. "It's not like you've gotta take him in the bathroom or anything, he's a big kid. Besides, it'll be a good chance for me and the Captain here to have a chat."

Lauren searches her sister's face and then mine, "Okay," she answers slowly. "I guess we'll meet you guys over at the picnic tables," she puts her hand on Chris's shoulder lightly and guides him away, shooting her sister one last look of suspicion before walking away with our son.

"Let's go get some pizza!" Chelsea smiles at me and gives my arm a tap to bring me back from watching Lauren's perfect ass swing away.

"Sure," we walk past long lines of exhausted parents and their endless pits of energy for kids and make our way over to the food trucks.

"Hey, this was a great idea, by the way. I think Lauren needed some down time and Chris is having a blast," Chelsea seamlessly threads her way past the oncoming crowd. I've gotta admit, being surrounded by so many people has been tugging at my nerves all day. Now that it's noon, the park is packed and I can feel my blood pressure going up as the free space shrinks closer around me.

I've never loved huge crowds, but Afghanistan solidified my contempt. Over there, being surrounded by groups of people meant that extra diligence was needed. Constant surveying of the markets or busy streets for signs of danger or hostility. Over there, heavy crowds meant watching your men get attacked in a cowardly ambush. Over there, too many people swarming around meant death.

"I'm happy that they're happy," it's not a lie. It's the reason I've been fighting my instinct to get the fuck outta here every time another gaggle of strange faces has put me on edge.

"Yeah, I can see that. It's good that you're trying to make her happy, Mack. I mean, Lauren has had it rough for a long time now.

I'm sure you're aware." She shoots me a pointed look that instantly pulls me from my battle with claustrophobia and makes me feel like I'm not towering over her. Damn, that dirty look must run in the family. Her and her sister have it down pat. "I mean, because when you took off on her ten years ago, it didn't seem like you were really thinking about her happiness then," she continues. Twist the knife, why don't ya?

"I wanted to stay with her back then too, she wasn't having it," I shoot back, but somehow with Chelsea giving me the side eye, I don't have as much conviction in my voice.

"Yeah, you were both a dumb couple of kids," she agrees. "And I can see you've changed. You grew up into a great man. A man that would be a powerful influence on Chris's life," she continues.

"Thanks," I follow her as she weaves past an elderly couple walking about a quarter mile an hour. The smell of food tells me that we're near the trucks before my eyes do. A mixture of scents perfume the air; the concoction is similar to the clash of spices at the market in Afghanistan. My vision blurs and suddenly sand grits under my feet where asphalt was only a second ago. The heat of the Afghani sun is searing my skin and beads of sweat break out on my forehead. I blink hard and take a deep breath. Focus. When I open my eyes, Chelsea is watching me closely. I must have stopped walking because we're both standing still.

"You ok?" she peers at me like a child looking at a bug they're seeing for the first time.

"Yeah, for sure. Just, uh, got dizzy for a sec. I'm good."

"Ok," she looks at me with one eyebrow cocked. "Well, let's get some slices. Maybe you need some food." She nods over at the pizza truck and we get in the line for food.

"Anyway, I'm not trying to give you a hard time or anything," Chelsea picks up where she left off.

"You sure about that?" I look her straight in the eyes, not because of our conversation, but because it helps me stay focused on the present.

"I am. I'm actually trying to give you your props. I can see you've got a good heart and good intentions for my sister. I believe that people can change for the better and you've clearly done that."

"Thanks, I actually have a plan for later," I reach into my pocket.

"Hey, I don't need to know what you plan to do with her later. We're not that close!" she laughs and crinkles her nose the same way Lauren does.

"No, not that. Well ..." I shrug, "that too."

"Ewww." She sticks out her pink tongue. "Can I get four slices of pepperoni and four cans of coke?" She diverts her attention to the man waiting to take our order.

He nods and I drop the velvet box in my fingers and take out my wallet instead. I hand the guy some bills and Chelsea thrusts the cans of coke at me as she balances the giant slices of pizza in her hands.

"Anyway, my plan is to propose. So you don't need to worry about my intentions or me walking away anymore. I know you're just doing your job as a big sister, and I appreciate that Chelsea."

The truth is, Chelsea has always looked after Lauren in one way or another, even since we were all kids. I remember when I was seven and I pulled all the heads off Lauren's Barbie dolls and tossed them in the mud. Lauren cried like I had killed actual people and Chelsea chased me out of the yard with a skipping rope. And I don't mean she gently skipped over to me and asked me to leave. I mean she looped that rope over her hand and swung it at me like a whip. She was never one to mess with, even when she was nine.

She stops in her tracks and her brown eyes go wide. "You're proposing? Seriously? Oh my God, that's awesome!" She haphazardly tries to throw her pizza filled hands around me in an awkward hug.

"Thanks," I smile and pat her back with the cold coke cans in my hand.

"Ok, we're good now for sure," she beams at me. "Let's find some seats and keep an eye out for them," she scans the picnic tables in front of us, littered with bodies and fast food. "Oh, wait! Have you ever seen this guy?" Chelsea points toward one of the food trucks with her elbow. "You've got to see this, it's amazing!" She takes off in the direction of the truck with a sign that says "Fruit Ninja" on the side.

I guess the table is going to have to wait. I wade my way through the crowd toward the display and fight the anxiety climbing up my throat.

Chelsea and I come to a standstill in a group of onlookers at the side of the truck. The man behind the counter is a middle aged white dude with a martial arts belt tied around his head, Karate kid style.

Um, ok. What the fuck?

On the butcher block in front of him is a grapefruit, watermelon, pineapple and other fruit.

"What's the deal?" I ask Chelsea.

"He makes frozen yogurt with that stuff, but just watch, this is cool. I saw him on that food truck show on Food Network."

My eyes settle back on the fruit ninja as he takes in a deep breath and leans down under the counter to grab something. Suddenly he pops back up with a Japanese Katana sword in his hands. The blade glints in the sun as he lifts it up over his head. "Hi-eee-ah!" he shouts, swinging it down, splitting the pineapple in two.

The crowd around me erupts into clapping and cheers. Someone bumps into my elbow and I drop the cans of coke on the ground.

Oh *shit*.

I can't tear my eyes away even as I watch the blade thicken and transform before my eyes. The sleek sword grows short and crude as it turns into an ax in his hands.

Fuck.

"Hi-eee-ah!" he screams, the ax chops down into the grapefruit and I stare in disbelief as the belt around the man's head twists up into a turban. His white skin tans darker before my eyes and his little chin sprouts a salt and pepper beard.

I freeze. My throat burns dry and I can't speak. The food truck disappears and the sand returns. I'm back at the Shura again.

He lifts the ax back up again and yells loudly, "No!" I manage, but it's too late. I watch as the blade sinks into Thompson's head, the blood dripping down over his lips as the pink of his brain is exposed to the air.

I force my feet to move, the asphalt reappears under my shoes as I instinctively hurdle myself to the side of a garbage can. The bile rises in my throat and I puke into the can, grasping onto the sides for support. Wiping my mouth with the back of my hand, I look back over my shoulder at the scene. The fruit ninja truck reappears and on the block is a watermelon cut in two. Not my corporal's head.

People I've never met stare at me and judge, but I don't care. Fuck people.

"Shit, are you ok? What happened?" Chelsea swoops up beside me.

"Yeah," I lie. "I'm good, I uh, I guess that roller coaster did more of a number on me than I thought." I try to sound convincing.

"Really? We should probably get Chris and Lauren and get you back to the hotel then."

"No!" She steps back and peers up at me. "Sorry, I just don't want to ruin such a nice day. I'm fine, I really am. I'm just not as young as I used to be, can't take those crazy rides anymore I guess." My voice has more conviction now. I almost believe myself. "Plus, I still want to take Lauren on the Ferris wheel. That's where I want to propose. I swear, I'm fine, ok? Don't tell her about this, it'll just get her all worried again." I plead.

Chelsea bites her lip and searches my face for the truth. "Ok," she agrees finally. "Let's go find them. But no more roller coasters!" she chides.

"Cross my heart," I follow her toward the picnic tables.

I can promise that I won't go on anymore roller coasters, but how can I promise that this will never happen again?

I can't.

CHAPTER 32:

Year - 2014

Lauren

"We should probably get back to the hotel," I look at the sun sliding down in the sky, like a barometer for our energy levels after such a long day.

"Awww, but Mom, I'm not even tired," Chris yawns as soon as he utters the words. I can't help but laugh. He hasn't changed since he was in diapers. Always trying to get one more story or play just one more game before his bedtime.

"Well you might not be, but I am." I rub my hand over his short, black hair.

Mack doesn't say anything, he looks distracted. He's been acting kind of distant all afternoon. Ever since him and my sister went to get food. I know Chelsea wanted to talk to him about something, I just hope she didn't get under his skin. I know my big sister has the best of intentions and that she's fiercely protective of Chris and I, but she can come on a little strong.

"What do you think? Are you ready to get going?" I drop my voice and turn to look at Mack. He's so handsome. The way the sun is bouncing off his blue eyes and highlighting the tiny red hairs in his beard. He looks rugged. Sexy. I might be able to get a second wind when we get back to the hotel room. Even more inspiration to get this show on the road.

"Hmmm," he slowly shakes free from whatever thoughts are consuming him. "Go? Oh, no, I wanted to go on one more ride before we leave." He looks over at me and then quickly over to Chelsea.

"Jeez, you're just as bad as Chris," I chuckle. Of course he is. Like father like son.

"No, I mean, I want to take you on the Ferris wheel before we go. Just the two of us," his smile makes the corners of his eyes crinkle. How can I resist anything this man wants?

"Hey, bud," Chelsea cuts in, "whaddya say you and I head back to our room and watch some tv? I'll let ya order room service for some ice cream." She throws her arm around my son and gives him a little squeeze.

"Really? Yeah! Ok." Chris is easy to keep happy. I'm so happy I have my son back. The boy who is carefree and smiles easily.

"We'll see you two at breakfast tomorrow," Chelsea winks at me. At least I think it's at me. I get the feeling she may have meant it for Mack.

"Thanks," I smile back at her, but she's not paying attention to me. She is looking at Mack. What's that about? "Be good for your aunt and don't stay up too late, ok?" I put my arms on Chris's shoulders and give him as much of a hug as he'll allow in public anymore.

"Mom!" he groans, looking around self-consciously. I guess I've still managed to embarrass him.

"We'll be fine; you guys just enjoy your night." Chelsea finally looks at me and steers Chris toward the exit under her arm.

I watch them walk away and then turn to Mack. He looks so good in the rosy hue that the setting sun is casting on his skin. I mean, he looks good in any hour of the day, but the golden hour was given that name for a reason. Desire prickles over me and I throw my arms over his shoulders and stand on my tippy-toes to give him a quick kiss.

"You know; we could head back to the hotel too. I'm not interested in watching a movie, but I think I can keep you entertained," I murmur against his cheek.

"I'm going to take you up on that," he slides his hand across my lower back and presses me tight to his hard body. "Right after we go on the Ferris wheel together."

Seriously?

"Um, ok. I guess." I'll admit it, I'm pouting a little. How can going on a dumb ride be more important that us getting naked together?

"Oh come on, put that lip away," he smiles and gives me a squeeze. "I've known you since you were six and we've never ever gone on a single ride together. Let's just do one spin on the wheel and then I'll take you on a different kind of ride," his voice deepens and my pussy clenches at the thought.

"Well since you put it that way," I step back and hold his hand, "lead the way."

As we cross the park grounds hand-in-hand, I remember how we used to walk around our high school at lunchtime like this. I was so proud to be the one on Mack Forrester's arm, while all the jealous girls wished they were me. It feels like no time has passed between us as I feel the heat of his palm against mine, reassuring me that I'm still his girl.

We get to the line for the Ferris wheel and I'm happy to see that the crowd has thinned out enough that we'll be on the next ride. It's not that I don't want to spend time with Mack, I appreciate the sentiment and everything, but I have more urgent matters to tend to back at the hotel. Like the matter of removing all his clothes and worshipping every inch of his cut, strong body. Things like that.

"Wait here one sec, ok?" Mack smirks at me and let's go of my hand. He walks away before I answer him and I watch as he cuts to the front of the line and starts talking to the guy running the wheel.

What on earth is he doing?

The man in charge of the ride stands up and shakes Mack's hand vigorously. Mack pulls out his wallet and pulls out a bill, folding it over in his hand and presses it into the guy's hand, but the man refuses. He waves his hands at him like windshield wipers in a downpour. What is he up to now? The last time I saw Mack do something like this was on our prom night when he paid the guy in the garage at the Colorado golf club to use the golf cart. The two of them shake hands again and Mack walks back to me with swagger and a smile.

"What was that all about?" I eye him suspiciously.

"Nothing to worry about, just having a nice chat that's all." he teases me.

"Uh huh," I know Mack Forrester and I know when he's up to something. However, I don't have time to get it out of him because the line starts moving forward and we shuffle along to our spots on the ride.

As we reach the front of the line, where the man who runs the wheel stands, he looks over at Mack and gives him a friendly nod. We take our seat and pull the bar over our laps, locking it in place tight.

"I know you're up to something, Mack."

He opens his eyes wide, giving me his best attempt at an innocent look, "I have no idea what you're talking about."

"Uh huh."

The chair lurches backward and we start to spin up around the Ferris wheel. Whatever Mack's up to slips my mind as we climb to the top of what feels like the world and the vibrant pink splashes across the sky catch my eye. "Oh my God, the sunset is amazing from up here," I whisper and Mack tucks his arm around me.

Thunk!

Our seat comes to a dead halt as soon as we reach the summit of the ride. Are you kidding me? I look over at Mack, I guess I didn't have to wait long to learn his plan.

"Mack, if you think for one second that I'm going to have sex with you up here, you better think again," I whisper loudly.

He doesn't say a word; his eyes twinkle mischievously.

"There's seriously no way. Are you nuts?" I hiss nervously looking around.

"Lauren, calm down. That's not why I got him to stop the ride," he slips his hand into his pocket and pulls out a small box. Before I can process any of it, he flips the velvet lid open and pulls out a diamond ring.

"Oh, Mack!"

"Lauren, listen, I had big plans to bring you up here and tell you how you're more gorgeous than this sunset," he nods toward the deepening shades of pink and purple painted across the sky surrounding us. "And how those first stars you see coming out right now are nothing compared to the twinkle in your eyes. Don't get me wrong. That's true. But, really, I just want us to have memories of a lifetime worth of sunsets blurring together. I want you to take my name, to be my wife, to give me children. Well, more children. I want you. Forever."

"Oh, of course. Yes. Yes!" My voice wavers and I feel like I'm in a dream. Mack pulls the ring out of the box and grabs my hand, sliding the sparkling diamond down my finger.

"You're mine. Forever," he murmurs happily.

"Forever," I agree, resting my head on his shoulder I hold my hand up to the sky and admire my ring against the fading sunset. I want to take a mental photograph of this moment and remember it forever as the day that my life began again.

CHAPTER 33:

Year - 2014

Lauren

The elevator doors pop open on our floor and Mack scoops me up off the ground, cradling me in his arms.

"What are you doing?" I squeal, kicking my legs in the air lightly. I love how easily Mack can sweep me off my feet. Literally.

"I'm gonna carry the bride across the thresh hold," there's no mistaking the intention written all over his face. If I was a wounded gazelle, I'd be nervous to see an animal look down on me like this. But what Mack doesn't know yet is that I'm no gazelle. I'm a lion.

"We're not married yet," I fake a protest. Honestly, I hope he doesn't put me back on my feet. I love being in his arms.

Mack stops in front of our room door and effortlessly adjusts me in his hold as he fishes the card for the door out of his pocket.

Sch-wick. Beep! The door swings open for us. Mack walks through and kicks it shut with his prosthetic leg.

He's come a long way, even in the short time span he spent at Spalding. His movements are so graceful now, he's mastered the nuances of balancing on one leg, or carrying women to bed. I bet he'll be ready to ride his motorcycle again soon. The idea floods me with a new wave of desire. The idea of his sitting on his bike, with a leather jacket and his tattoos peeping out from under the collar.

Why are we still wearing clothes right now?

"It might not be our wedding night yet," Mack walks me to the end of the bed and tosses me onto it, "but, I'm gonna fuck you like we're on our honeymoon."

"Isn't that what you did on the weekend?" My eyes travel greedily over him as he unbuttons his shirt. He slides it down over his shoulders and one by one his tattoos make an appearance. Each a symbol for a moment in his life I wasn't there for. As much as I love his ink, it hurts to see the marks of time we never had together permanently etched into his skin.

"The weekend was a nice test drive," he drops his shirt to the floor behind him, "but now I'm gonna ride ya like I stole ya." His blue eyes glint under the low light and my heart whooshes in my ears.

"Stand up here," Mack reaches forward and tugs my hand so I can get my feet under me on the bouncy bed. "I've got a good view from here," he smirks up at me.

"Of what?" I look down at him and steady myself on the bed.

"Of you stripping for me, sweetheart." He lets go of my hand and turns around, grabbing the little chair at the desk across the room. Dragging it to the end of the bed, he takes a seat and looks up at me expectantly.

I've never stripped for anyone before. Joel was a good man, but he was not very exciting in bed. I feel a little silly, but the fire in Mack's eyes helps me find my courage. "I don't have any music," I say tossing out my best excuse.

"Well, let me fix that for you then." Mack stands and turns on the tv to the music station. Nicki Minaj appears on the screen in hot pink spandex while Sir Mix-A-Lot's voice gives me some inspiration. "My anaconda don't want none unless you got buns, hun."

Mack sits back down in his seat, "Perfect song for you." He smiles up at me.

Ok. I got this.

I swivel my hips and fall straight back onto my big butt, and I cannot lie ... it's embarrassing. I look past the laugh that Mack's trying to suppress over his shoulder at the tv. On the screen, Nicki is on all fours, making Drake re-evaluate his life as she shakes her ass.

Alright, I got this.

I quickly pull my shirt over my head and throw it over Mack's face.

"Hey, what are you doing?" He pulls the shirt down and I'm on my back squirming out of my pants.

"You don't get to speak. You get to watch," I purr, dropping my jeans onto the floor beside the bed. Mack's stifled laugh evaporates into the air and his eyes narrow, but I've got his attention.

I flip over onto my hands and knees, facing the headboard, so my thick curves are on display for Mack. Leaning down onto my elbows, I pop my ass in the air and shimmy my hips until my round cheeks are trembling to the beat. I look over my shoulder and Mack is silent. He looks like he's under a spell. A surge of confidence charges through me and I crawl forward on the bed, slowly, stretching my legs out. Then I push myself back, until I'm at the very edge of the bed, my ass shaking and my pussy only inches from Mack's face.

From his mouth.

I drop my head back to the comforter again, my ass still trembling, and press my ear flat against the bed. I push my breasts down onto the mattress so my ass is accentuated even more. I can feel Mack's breath on the inside of my thighs, my pussy growing wet with desire.

"Don't move," Mack growls. Before I have a chance, I feel his strong hands on my hips, pining me in place. He leans forward until his lips are brushing the edge of my panties, and grazes his teeth across my skin as he bites the edge of them and tugs them down over my ass until my pussy is exposed to the air.

I breathe into the comforter, my chest pressing into the mattress every time I fill my lungs. Suddenly, Mack's warm tongue snakes between my lips and quickly finds my aching clit. His nose presses in between my cheeks as he buries his face in my ass. He cups his tongue up over my clit and then flattens it out, making me moan and twist the comforter in my fingers.

Mack's hands drop from my hips and his fingers slide up between my thighs, digging into my flesh, he opens me wide for him until it's almost painful. Lucky for me, he's there to kiss it all better. His lips surround my clit and his soft tongue flickers over me relentlessly, all I can do is groan as the pleasure wracks my body.

"Oh fuck, don't stop!" I cry out. Ecstasy floods my body, like a star exploding into a supernova, it ripples out from my pussy and rushes through me. My toes are curled and my fingers are twisted in cloth as my eyes roll back and I cry out.

Mack moves away from me, and I'm frozen in place. No man has ever made me feel like he does. I feel like a goddess being worshipped on his tongue.

It's time to return the favor.

I sit back up and blood rushes to my head. When I stop seeing stars, I turn around and Mack is standing in front of the chair now, completely naked.

God damn, he's big. His thick cock is ready for me, swaying slightly under it's own weight.

Sliding off the end of the bed, I stand up in front of him and kick off my panties that are still tangled half way down my thighs.

"You need to sit back down," I instruct him. "I'm not done my show yet." I push him lightly and he plops back down on the chair. "Oh, what do you have in mind?" he murmurs. But I won't tell him, I'll show him. I slip between his thighs and slide down onto my knees in front of my man. His prosthetic leg is cool against my skin on the one side and in striking contrast to the soft warmth radiating from his other leg. I remember when we had sex at my house, it took a bit to adjust to the new sensation, but I love it.

Mack has been my hero since we were young and he punched Benjamin Reed right in the nose for pushing me into a mud puddle. I remember how devastated I was as the dirty water soaked up into my pastel yellow dress and how Mack pulled me to my feet and set Benjamin straight. I couldn't help but smile when he wiped away my tears with his swollen knuckles. I knew then that he was my hero for life.

His leg is just a physical reminder of how I now have to share my hero with the rest of America.

His cock is so close to my lips; I can feel the heat of his skin. Sticking my tongue out, I lick a long trail from the base of his cock, slowly up to the tip. I look him in the eyes as I swipe my tongue over his most sensitive part and he groans, watching me closely. Opening wide, I take him in my mouth, his cock sliding down along my tongue until he reaches my throat. The last time he went in my mouth this deep, I gagged. This time, I'm relaxed and in control of my reflexes as I push down past my comfort until my lips are circling the base of his cock.

"Oh, damn," he gasps.

I bob my head, letting his thick member slide across my tongue and into my throat over and over. It's a little slower than using my hands and mouth together, but I don't think either of us is in a rush. We have all night.

"Stand up," Mack's voice is hoarse.

I guess maybe one of us is in a rush after all.

I let his cock fall free from my lips and pull myself back up to my feet again.

"Good girl, now turn around, I want to see your sweet ass bouncing when I fuck you." His hands guide my hips as I turn around, easing me down onto his thick member. I'm so wet from him making me cum that he slides into me a bit easier this time. I push my ass all the way down until I'm sitting on his lap and his cock is fully inside me.

Using the arms of the chair and more strength in my thighs than I knew I had, I ride Mack like a cowgirl bucking around on the back of a bull. Mack's hands wrap around me, grabbing my tits as my pussy clenches around him tight.

"God, Lauren, you look so fucking good," he murmurs in my ear. Suddenly he lurches me forward and I flop down onto the bed, face first, without warning. In a second, Mack is standing behind me, between my legs as I'm bent over the bed.

"What are you doing?" I'm surprised by him tossing me around like a rag doll, but I'm not upset. It's kind of fucking hot.

"I told you, I'm going to ride you like I stole ya," his hand wraps up around my throat and he pulls my head up off the bed as he thrusts his cock back into my pussy in one swift stroke. I groan at the sensation of being filled by him. Mack's hand is holding my face up toward the ceiling under my chin, my back is arched back and I'm completely under his control. His thrusts get quicker and I moan as he fucks me, hard.

I can feel my body building up with pleasure as Mack takes what's his. Suddenly my body stiffens under him as another orgasm rolls through me. The last one was hot and intense like an explosion, but this one is slower and the bliss is more thorough like a warm fire on a cold night.

Mack fucks me harder and all I can hear is the sound of our bodies slapping together, he jerks behind me and his movements grow erratic as he fills me with his cum. Mack drops his hand from my chin and I fall over onto the bed, happy to lie in the wake of my ecstasy.

He joins me on the mattress, pulling me up against him so my legs aren't dangling over the edge anymore. He pulls me against him until my head is lying on his chest and his heartbeat is the only thing I can hear.

"I love you, Lauren," he whispers into my hair.

I feel like I've finally found my happy ending. I'm engaged to the one man I've always loved from childhood until now. To Chris's father. To my hero. To Mack Forrester.

"I love you too," I whisper back. I can feel sleep drifting over me, taking me into a land of dreams. I'll rest easy knowing that everything has finally worked out for me. For us. And that we'll never be torn apart again.

CHAPTER 34:

Year - 2014

Mack

"Because you know I'm all about that bass, 'bout that bass. No treble!" Lauren and Chelsea sing along to the hottest hit of the moment up in the front while the little man and I ride in the back. It's nice to see Lauren having fun and letting loose for once. Having these past few days off have been good for her.

"Yeah, it's pretty clear, I ain't no size two." Lauren and Chelsea look at each other with huge smiles as they belt out the words. "But

I can shake it, shake it, like I'm supposed to do." Lauren looks back at me and winks.

Can she ever. She proved that in the hotel. Damn, I still can't get the image of her on all fours, shaking her fat ass for me out of my head. I'm not sure I ever want to. I always knew that she had a wild streak in her, but back in high school I was just so relieved when she finally let me fuck her. I was happy to have the same clumsy, missionary sex over and over. Now, it looks like she could teach me a thing or two.

I look over at Chris, but he's got his head resting against the window and his eyes closed. Smart kid. I wish I could get some shut-eye too, but after my time in the army, I've just never been able to relax on long drives anymore. Driving off the base, on long stretches of highway, is one of the most dangerous things you can do in a war zone. It's the perfect opportunity for the enemy to surround your vehicle and open fire. We've lost more good men and women that way than I'd care to count.

Instead I stare out the window and try to relax. I should probably be trying to figure out my next move. Where I'm going to live, for instance. Lauren offered that I stay with her. Move in. I want to, but I'm just not sure if that's too fast for Chris. The last thing I want to do is start our time as a family off on a sour note. I want him to be comfortable with me in his life.

Will Lauren ever tell Chris that I'm his father? How will he take it? I keep wondering how we're going to approach that minor detail. And by minor detail, I mean life altering revelation. I suppose

I should focus on one thing at a time though. Figure out the living situation first, the rest will follow.

The sing along comes to an end and the news update comes on. "A tragedy today as we lost another soldier to an improvised explosive device in Afghanistan. With only three months left until our troops are finally withdrawn from the war, the loss of nineteen-year-old Private Beckett is particularly painful ..."

"Turn it off," Chelsea hisses at Lauren and jerks her head back toward me. Lauren quickly hits the button and the vehicle goes silent.

"You don't need to do that, I'm fine." But my voice won't lie for me. My tone tells them the truth. They know how hard it is for me to hear about another of my brothers in arms losing his life over there.

Nineteen. Jesus, I'm almost a decade older than him. He was just a kid.

My eyes go back to the window and billows of dust waft past us. Chelsea slows the SUV down a bit as an orange sign informs us that we're getting jammed up by construction. Damned road work, why don't they just do repairs at night when most people aren't out driving? I've never understood that. Instead, they tie up the roads with inconvenient traffic when everyone is rushing to get some-where. Makes perfect sense.

"Is there a detour you can take or something?" I try to disguise the edge in my tone. My palms are beginning to sweat a bit at the thought of being stalled for too long.

"A detour? No, we've just gotta wait," Chelsea slows down to a crawl as we near the stopped cars ahead of us. The road has been reduced to one lane and they're letting the on coming traffic take their turn.

"Great," I mutter, rubbing my hands together.

Outside my window, the dust from the gravel and dirt on the dug up road ahead is blowing around. It reminds me of the dust ups we used to deal with everyday in Afghanistan. Man I don't miss those, the grains of sand whipping against my face like a million tiny razor blades. I instinctively rub my hand over the side of my face and narrow my eyes. Even though the swirling dirt is outside the window, the reaction is automatic.

"Wow, look at the huge trucks," Lauren looks out the windshield as the ground beneath our tires begin to rumble and shake. Massive dump trucks travel toward us, carrying broken asphalt and rocks.

"They're noisy," Chelsea complains, raising her voice to be heard over them.

I close my eyes for a second and fight the panic I can feel rising up the back of my throat. Breathe. This is a construction zone, not a war zone. Just breathe. I look back out my window and feel prickles of sweat tingle my hairline as the oversized yellow trucks fade into battered old busses. The windows are covered with black plastic garbage bags so you can't see inside them.

"Move! We've got to go! Come on!" I order, but my man at the wheel doesn't move. "Why aren't you going? We're being swarmed!"

"I can't move," the voice is distant, like a bad transmission on a radio. "The guy in front of me isn't moving!"

"We don't have time for this. We've gotta get out of here." I pop the door open on our Humvee and jump out. The sand clouds around my boots as I march over to the driver in our convoy who is deciding to risk everyone's lives while the enemy is approaching.

"What are you doing?" I bang on his window. "Drive! Now! You're gonna get us all killed!" I slam my open palm against the glass and the driver jumps up straight and looks at me. "Don't just fucking look at me, I said to get in gear and go. We're going to get swarmed! Don't you see the busses coming?"

He doesn't do anything, the insubordinate bastard. Maybe he's afraid. They say some guys freeze up at the weirdest times. This guy couldn't have chosen a worse one. I pop the handle on his door and grab him by his uniform, my face an inch from his. "Listen to me, you need to move or we're all going to be killed! Do you hear me? Get this truck in gear now!" I yell. His co-navigator starts yelling too, but I can't make out the words.

The driver just stares at me; he's clearly not going to get this vehicle out of the way. I can't lose my men like this. I've got to do something. Fast. I reach over and unclick his seat belt and pull him out of the Humvee. If he won't move this truck, I will. I climb in and my stomach lurches.

The woman next to me. Where did she come from? I look around and the Humvee I was sitting in seconds ago has disappeared. Instead, I'm in a minivan. Terror grips my heart and my chest feels like it's being crushed as the woman's screams finally penetrate my ears.

"Oh my God, please, please! Don't hurt us! Please! Let us go. You can have the van, just let me and the kids go!" she yelps.

I look in the rear view mirror at the crying children in the back bench seat. What is happening?

"Get out of the car and put your hands on your head!" A man barks at my side. I look over, and a cop is standing a foot away from me with his gun drawn and pointing at my head.

Fuck.

"I said, get out of the car, sir!" he repeats himself and I comply, slowly sliding out of the seat until my feet hit the pavement below me. I put my hands flat on my head and am instantly tackled to the ground. My arms are wrenched behind my back and the cold pinch of metal surrounds my wrists.

I'm easily lifted by two men back onto my feet and I see the red and blue lights flashing on the police car for the first time. Everything still feels unreal. Like this is a dream. This can't be real. I just blink and wait for my mind to wake up, but it won't.

Looking around, I can see that people are standing outside of their cars with their cellphones held out at the end of their arms. Their faces are contorted with horror and fascination.

"Mack!" I snap my head toward Lauren's voice and see her on the side of the road, bawling. Under her arm is Chris, his face is pushed into her ribs. Chelsea is next to them both, glaring at me.

"Watch your head, sir. One of the officers pushes down on my scalp and I duck into the back seat of the cruiser. He slams the door shut in my face and outside the window I can still see Lauren screaming my name.

This isn't a dream. This is a fucking nightmare.

CHAPTER 35:

Year - 2014

Lauren

How is it that I'm parked at yet another police department to pick up yet another one of my guys? Mack was told that he's free to go after being detained for a couple of hours. He called and asked me to pick him up. Of course I said yes, but not because I'm happy to do so. Him and I need to have a serious talk. Things have gotten out of control.

Mack must have spotted me when I pulled in here, because he's quickly crossing the parking lot toward my car. From his casual strut and easy smile, you'd never know he was the same guy who dragged a poor man out of his car in a terrifying melt down this morning.

He opens the door and ducks his head down to look over at me. "Hey gorgeous, thanks for springing me from the joint," he teases, his eyes sparkling.

"Get in, Mack." My voice is like a flat line on a heart monitor. My happiness isn't far behind it.

Mack's smile turns down at the corners as he closes his mouth, but he doesn't push it. He slides into the passenger seat and closes his door with a thud.

"How about we go out for dinner? I'll buy us a nice bottle of wine and then I can make this all up to you when we get back home. Your sweet nectar can be my dessert," his eyes narrow and his voice drops low.

He's so sexy. I could lose all of my senses, my sight, my hearing, my smell, and still know that. It would still radiate from him and permeate my soul. The idea of his face buried between my thighs is certainly enough to distract me for a second.

But, it's never going to be enough to fix what happened today.

"Mack, we have to talk," his smirk slips off his face and he refuses to look at me. Instead, he pushes his jaw out as he stares straight ahead.

"Lauren, look, I know things got a bit crazy today, but it's all going to be fine. The police didn't think it was a big enough deal to press any charges, so I don't think we need to rehash it."

If this was a foreign film, the subtitle underneath him would be two words long: Drop It.

Part of me wants to let it go. To believe that this was just a one-off situation. That nothing needs to change.

That part of me is a fucking liar.

"No, Mack. We do need to rehash it 'cause this can't keep happening. Do you even remember what you did today? Do you remember dragging a father out of his vehicle in front of his wife and kids and trying to drive away? Because that's a scene I don't think I'm going to ever forget."

Mack's eyebrows furrow together like storm clouds rolling in across a darkening sky. I watch his face for a flicker of recognition. For some small sign that he does remember, but the vacant, million-mile stare in his eyes tells me he doesn't.

"The police filled me in on it," he finally mumbles.

His eyelids look heavy; like he hasn't slept in days. It's clear that he hasn't left the war behind. He may have escaped Afghanistan with his life, but his soul is still trapped over there, a POW being slowly tortured to death.

"Mack, I …" my mind searches. I want to be gentle with him. I want to find the right words to say what I need to. However, I know he'll just smell the bullshit through the flowers. "I want you to get help. I want you to go to therapy."

"No." There's no anger attached to his voice, but his single word hits me like a sucker punch to the gut.

"Mack, please, just listen."

"No, you listen," he drops his head and his voice is barely a whisper. "There's nothing wrong with me. I don't need some quack analyzing me and asking me whether or not I loved my mother. I'm a soldier, Lauren. I've been to war and I watched my men die. I have bad days, that's the way that goes. I don't need to go to some Kumbaya preaching, hug-me sessions to know that."

"Look, I'm not a doctor, ok? So, I'm not going to pretend I can diagnose you or anything, but I think you might have PTSD, Mack." He puffs out his chest and his lips twist in protest. "There's no shame in that!" I quickly add, trying to smooth over the blow to his ego. "Hell, after what you've gone through, it would be more shocking if you didn't have some kind of residual scars that need healing. I just want what's best for you, and our family. I can't have you walking around like a ticking time bomb in Chris's life."

"Don't talk to me about bombs, Lauren. I've seen enough of them go off. You're the one blowing this whole thing out of proportion. I'm not gonna go sit on some therapist's couch just because I had a bad day. It's not happening. End.Of.Fucking.Story." He slams his fist into his palm with every punctuated word.

A huge part of me just wants to let that be the end of the story. Our son's face as he watched Mack in a fit of confusion and rage is burned into my brain though. I can't let this be the end of the story. Chris needs stability, he needs a father, and Mack is in no position to be either.

"It's not just one bad day, Mack, and you know it. Chelsea told me about what happened by the fruit truck, ok? I know about that.

Chris told me about how you got shaky at the grave. Mack, you even threw me to the ground that day at the track. Do you remember? I thought you were just trying to screw around, but I've been thinking about it a lot. It was because of that car that back fired, wasn't it? It's not just one thing, or one day. It's getting worse and I can't let this become everyday of our lives."

I reach across the car and place my hand on his. He peers up at me, just like his son does when he needs reassurance. Am I getting through to him?

Suddenly, he flings my hand off of his like it's a mosquito about to bite. No. No, I'm not.

"You said it yourself, you are not a doctor, Lauren. You're not a therapist. The last time I checked, you were a nurse. So, how about you let the big boys do their job and you worry about yours, ok?" His eyes flicker with rage and his face burns crimson. "For the last time, there's nothing wrong with me. I'm not some delicate flower, got it? I don't need to sit around and cry about my feelings. And I'm not going to fucking therapy!" He spits out the last words like they're tainted in poison.

Silence builds like a tidal wave, drowning us.

"Fine." I find my voice and look down at the steering wheel. "If you won't get help, then you need to leave. I can't take you to my place, Mack." Tears sting my eyes as I realize what I have to do.

"What are you talking about? Are you trying to blackmail me?"

"Blackmail? No. This is an ultimatum. You either get the help you need, or you can't be in our lives anymore. I can't always be wondering and waiting for you to explode again. This time you pulled an innocent man out of his car. Do you know how upsetting it was for Chris to see that today? What are you going to do next time? Beat someone to death? No. You either get help, or you leave." My voice wavers, but my mind is made up.

Silence again. It hurts my ears more than anything Mack could yell or say. I keep staring at the wheel, hoping that Mack will listen to reason. That he'll put his family, not to mention his health, above his inflated ego and pig-headedness.

"Fine," he sighs.

Oh, thank you God. I silently pray. Thank you!

Mack reaches over to the door and opens it, stepping back outside of the car before I fully understand what's happening. "Then, I'm leaving." He slams the door in my face and storms back to the police station as I watch in disbelief.

Mack Forrester had only just walked back into my life a little over a week ago, and now he's leaving me again. And this time, I think it's for good.

CHAPTER 36:

Year - 2014

Mack

The oak table under my arm is solid and the beer in my glass is frosty cold. Both sensations are keeping me grounded in the present. After what happened on the drive today I know being grounded is just what I need. Lauren's furrowed brows and soft eyes linger in my mind and all of a sudden I don't want to be grounded anymore. I want to be fucking drunk.

The pub is pretty much a ghost town at only four in the afternoon with the exception of the bartender, a young couple laughing in a booth and a slovenly drunk guy who's cozied up to the bar like it's a replacement for the wife that surely left him.

Across from me, the twenty-four-hour news station is passing off their opinion as facts. The news anchors keep yelling at each other like children competing for their mother's attention. They discuss every point like it all has the same weight, whether is about a drunk driving accident or Kim and Kanye, the fervour is the same.

"Are high-tops the new flip-flops in hip hop? Find out about this summer's latest fashion craze coming up in the next hour." The voiceover tries to titillate us with the hard hitting stories coming up. Seriously? Is this the news or Dr. *fucking* Seuss? It's annoying and little more than a background noise. Until my face flashes on the flat screen.

Oh, that ain't good.

Of course, they're using my military grad picture where I'm in full dress uniform. How long do you have to be out of the military before they stop using those pictures? Five years? Ten?

My mind flashes back to my first day at West Point, when Staff Sergeant Skillnick formed us up in our civvies and gave us his introductory speech. "Welcome to West Point, ladies and gentlemen. Let me make it clear to you, that will be the last time anyone in your life refers to you that way. From now on, no matter what you do. No matter where you go. You will always be known for your military service first. It's an honor few are ever awarded and not one to be taken lightly. So just remember this, whether you're buying your first house or getting arrested for your first crime, it will be you rank, your service and this United States military that will open those doors for you, or that you will tarnish with your bad decisions. Choose carefully."

Fuck.

My attention snaps back up to the television and I strain to listen to the same newscasters that only moments ago I was hoping would choke to death on live tv.

The blonde with the severe make-up and over processed hair jumps in, "clearly, Captain Forrester has lost it." She shares her unbiased, professional view. "Have you seen the video footage?" She drawls. "It's just disgraceful. In my opinion he should have to give back the medals he was awarded. A man like that shouldn't get to keep the highest award for courage..."

"Hey," I interrupt the program and wave my hand at the bartender. "Do you mind turning the channel?"

The guy behind the counter doesn't even look up from his phone. He just picks up the remote and clicks it one channel higher to an afternoon cooking show.

"Hey, man. Sorry I'm running behind," Cameron Armstrong comes up behind me and plops down on the chair across from me. "Have you been waiting here long?" He looks down at the beer I'm one swig away from finishing.

"Nah, I've just had the one," I hold up the bottle and finish the last mouthful.

"Ok, well, I'll get us a couple more." He pops back up out of the chair and heads over to the bar.

How about a couple dozen more?

I distract myself by peeling at the label of my empty Stella and Cameron clunks two more down on the table and shimmies out of his jacket, hanging it on the back of his chair. "I'm glad you called, man," he looks at me earnestly. "I was hoping we could get some drinks sometime."

"Thanks for coming out. I know it's on short notice." I lift up the new bottle and tilt it toward him in a silent salute.

"I didn't have much going on today anyway, so this is perfect." His jacket erupts with a sound of bubbles surfacing on water and Cameron reaches into the pocket and pulls out his cellphone. "Shit, sorry about that," he swipes his thumb across it and a huge pair of brown titties fills his screen in a text message. "I forgot to set it to vibrate. I'll do that now," he leaves the tits and changes his settings.

"Looks like you've got it pretty rough there, Armstrong," I nod to the phone. "A hard knock life, huh?"

My old Corporal shrugs it off. "You know how it is, all these girls are all flash and no substance. Not like what you've got with that Lauren chick. That shit looks like the real deal." He chucks his phone back in his pocket and takes a long gulp of his beer.

Twist the knife, why don't ya?

Instead of getting into any of that mess, I just down another third of my beer.

"You know, it's the craziest thing," he continues, looking down the neck of his bottle, "I've got all this easy poon chasing me left and right, but I haven't been able to get Lauren's sister out of my head since the game. Did she, uh, mention me at all?" He looks up at me.

"Huh? Oh, no. Not to me anyway. Her and I aren't really close or anything."

His mouth twists to the side like he's in deep thought. "Hey man, do you think you could bring her to another game for me? Or, maybe give her my number?"

"Seriously? Armstrong, what are we? In high school? Do you want me to pass her a note in science class too?" Irritation is sewn through my words like the lace on one of Mr. Star Quarterback's footballs.

"Jeez man, who pissed in your cornflakes?" He frowns at his bottle and I watch a wave of realization wash over his face. "Oh, uh, you know what? You're right. My bad, man. I know it's been a shit day for you." He looks up from his drink sheepishly.

I sigh. Obviously he knows about the incident today. I guess everyone knows. That's a hard pill to swallow. "No, don't worry about it," I wave my hand like I'm trying to sweep away the bad vibes. "I'm just being pissy cause Lauren and I broke up."

Cameron slowly swallows the beer in his mouth, and his eyebrows shoot sky high as he looks over at me. "I didn't know, that sucks man."

"Yeah, I'm just trying to figure out what to do. I thought I might be living at her place, but now I need to figure out a 'Plan B' I guess."

"You'll stay with me." Cameron quickly interjects. He's not asking me. It isn't an invitation, it's a statement.

"That's nice of you, but you don't have to do that. Trust me, that's not why I asked you to come out or anything."

"Fuck that. You're staying with me. It's done. You'll crash at my place as long as it takes to get yourself sorted out... uh, I mean settled." He looks up at me nervously.

"Thanks." Somehow the word feels too small for the gratitude I feel.

"Don't mention it," he shrugs it off. "It sounds like you've had one hell of a couple days. If staying at my place helps, it's all yours. I can never repay you for what you did for me, Captain. There's not a lot of men who would've risked their life like you did to save me. If crashing on my couch is something that can help you, then you can stay as long as you need." He states matter-of-factly.

"You're a good man, Armstrong." I take another drink of my girl Stella and she goes down easy, just like I like 'em.

"Don't mention it, but, Captain?" His eyes dart up to mine and he nervously licks his lips.

"Yeah?"

"I just want you to know that I'll help you in anyway I can. Like, if you need a hand tracking down someone to talk to or anything, I can help with that too.

"I don't need help, thanks." My words cover our conversation in frost.

Cameron picks at the label on his beer as the awkwardness marinates us. He looks torn. "I think you do." He finally answers, his voice is barely above a whisper, but the push back is undeniable.

"Listen, I don't need help," I stress for the third time today. "If this is the kinda strings your offer to stay with you comes with then forget it." I thump my bottle on the table and get up to leave. Where I'm going, I have no idea, but I'm not going to sit here and listen to this shit.

On the television the five o'clock news flashes on across the bar and a shaky cellphone video of earlier today leads the day's stories. I stop and watch in horror as I see myself, frantic, panicked and screaming at the poor man in the minivan to drive. The terror on my face in undeniable and my stomach flops like a fish on a line as I have the out of body experience of seeing myself pull the guy from his vehicle. "In today's top story," the crimson lipped news anchor somberly tells the camera, "Captain Mack Forrester, West Point graduate, and the famous hero veteran who lost his leg saving several lives in the Afghanistan war, was arrested for the scene you just witnessed."

I slump back down in my seat, defeated. I drag my fingers through my hair and down the back of my neck as I try to digest what I just watched.

Fuck.

I look up at Cameron, and swallow hard to try to shake this feeling like a dump truck just dropped a ton of bricks on me and left me for dead.

"Ok, man." I nod my head and close my eyes, forcing myself to say the words: "I need help."

CHAPTER 37:

Year – 2014

Lauren

My cellphone buzzes with another text from Chelsea. I've already ignored at least five phone calls from her on the home phone. Now she's blowing up my cell.

I pick it up from the coffee table and read her message: "call me. It's an emergency."

Someone better be critically injured or dead. Guilt instantly boils in my gut at the thought. I call my sister and it doesn't even get to a full ring before she answers.

"Lauren! Have you heard from Mack?" She sounds breathless.

"Chelsea are you seriously calling me every two seconds for this? I'm hanging up." What was moments ago guilt is now anger lapping it's flames up from my belly.

"No, wait! I don't mean about you two, I mean, have you seen that he's doing an interview? I sent you a link. He's talking to Cooper Sanders tomorrow and they're doing a live special. They never do the interviews live on CNB." She rambles.

I walk over to my computer and open the e-mail she sent me. Sure enough, there's a link to the CNB'S homepage. I click it and Mack's military photograph is staring into me. The same picture they've been using on the news all week. Just below is a YouTube video with an oversized play button in the middle of it. I don't need to click it; I've seen the footage of Mack's meltdown about a hundred times in the past few days. Hell, I've seen it so much that the grainy cellphone footage is almost replacing my actual memory of the event.

Chelsea is still blah-blahing about something or other, but I can't pay attention. My eyes scan the article below the video, she's right. Mack is doing an exclusive, live interview with Cooper Sanders tomorrow night.

"Do you think they're going to talk about us?" I can't tell if Chelsea sounds horrified by the idea or flattered. "Do you think he's going to explain what happened?" She continues.

"I couldn't tell you," I answer her glumly. One thing is certain though: I'll be tuning in to find out.

CHAPTER 38:

Year – 2014

Mack

"*I*'m just gonna dust a little powder on your nose, that's all. You don't want to look shiny on camera," The chick I banged in the back of a vehicle in Afghanistan leans over me and runs a fluffy makeup brush over my face. Her tits are popping out of the low V-neck of her shirt. "There, all done," she steps back and admires her work, blinking her long eyelashes.

She's pretty, that much is undeniable. Too bad looking into her eyes is like taking a glance down into the Grand Canyon. A barren, empty, seemingly bottomless void. What was it Cameron said the other night about these chicks? All flash and no substance.

Not like Lauren. My gut churns as I remember for the tenth time in the past hour the perfect woman I lost. Again.

"Thanks, uh..." there's no way this woman's name is coming back to me. Lauren would call her a card carrying member of my bimbo fan club, but I doubt she would appreciate the nickname. Although from the vapid stare she's returning, it might not bother her as much as you'd think.

"Tiffany," she fills in the blank cheerfully. From the way her face doesn't move at all, she's either full of Botox or she doesn't care that I forgot.

Probably both.

"Ok, let's get this stuff cleared out of here," Cooper walks over to the chair poised across from me to get ready for the interview. "Thanks Tiffany, you can go too," he directs her. She practically skips off the set, flipping her hair like she's in a shampoo commercial the whole way.

I can't believe I ever found girls like her sexy. Once you've been with a woman like Lauren, all you can see is how every other girl comes up short. Once you've had an exquisite work of art, paint by numbers just don't cut it anymore.

Cooper sits on the very edge of the chair across from me, holding a small stack of papers in his hands. His crew are buzzing all around us, checking wires and aiming cameras. I never realized how much went into these interviews. When he joined us in the desert, it was bare bones compared to this circus.

"Ok, so I just wanted to go over some of these questions with you so you know what to expect," he's hunched over with his elbows on his knees and barely speaking above a whisper. I get the feeling that he doesn't usually give his interview subjects a preview of the hard hitting questions he's known for serving up.

The cameras have been following me around all day, recording me being "natural". They've gotten footage of me cooking food, running with my blade, and of strangers recognizing me and thanking me for my service. I'm starting to feel like I'm in an infomercial selling portions of Captain "America" Mack Forrester.

But wait, if you act now they'll even throw in scenes of me petting puppies and kissing babies.

"Obviously, we're going to show the footage of the incident, ok? Then, I'm going to have to ask you if you think this is appropriate behaviour for a highly decorated war veteran. I know that sounds rough, but don't worry, I'm gonna follow up with a bit saying how you've had a hard go and that this is being blown out of proportion. Ok?" He looks up at me with his steely blue eyes and I can see that he's concerned for me.

He cares.

"You don't need to do that," I run my hand over my beard and try to ignore the voice inside telling me that this can all blow over, if I just let it. It looks like my old buddy Cooper Sanders is offering me a get out of jail free card. Wouldn't I be a fool to turn it down?

"The hell I don't!" He raises his voice and then looks around the studio self consciously. The two of us pop our heads up like a couple of groundhogs looking for shadows in February, but if any of his staff noticed him raise his voice they don't care enough to look our way.

"Come here," he leans into me, "look at this," he continues, rolling up the sleeve of his dress shirt until the lower half of his arm is exposed to me. "You see this?" His blue eyes settle on me.

"I can." I don't quite have a full sleeve of tattoos, but Cooper does.

His twisted scars mark a time I wish I could leave in the desert. A time that haunts my days, let alone my dreams. Down the entire length of his arm is a roadmap of the cowardly attack we both survived in Afghanistan.

"The plastic surgeons, they wanted to fix it. Make it disappear." He talks to me like he's revealing his deepest secret. "I told them to leave it alone. You know why?" His blue eyes always been hard to look away from. Never harder than now.

"Why?" The word somehow bubbles up from my lips.

"Because, when I went over there, to do the piece on you and the platoon, I thought I was king shit." He smiles sadly at the memory. "I thought I was at the top of my game. A hero, at least in journalism. That's why I pushed to keep up with you guys over there. I convinced myself I was just as badass as you guys, just without the uniform, you know?" He frowns and closes his eyes.

"Ok." I don't know what else to say? Do I tell him I'm sorry that Afghanistan ruined that for him? That me getting my leg blown off somehow sucked for him? Less words are often better, I'm learning.

"Yeah, that's what I thought. Until a grenade was thrown at my feet. Then I froze, didn't I?" He opens his eyes and looks straight at me like he wants me to confirm what he already knows. I nod but keep my mouth shut. "But, you didn't." He says with reverence. "You didn't even fucking hesitate. At all." He looks over his shoulders again, but no one cares about us any more than they did five minutes ago. "You saved my life," his blues suddenly look a little bluer when a mist forms around the bottom of his eyelids. "So, if I can return the favor, you better bet I will."

He sits up straight and pushes his shoulders back into the chair, looking at me like we're a couple of kids in a staring contest.

"Thank you," I finally answer, letting the gravity of what he's offering me to sink in. A second chance. Or is this three now? Either way, he's letting me off the hook, that much is clear.

"We're gonna roll in five minutes!" A disembodied voice yells to the side of us. Neither of us breaks our stare. I must not have been the only one who grew up with an older brother. This unblinking Olympics only hosts the most experienced and fierce of competitors.

"Got it," Cooper still doesn't break his stare, even as he runs the show. Gotta respect that shit.

Finally, I look away. Well, over his shoulder. I look into my past standing only a few feet away. Tiffany. Her full tits and her empty head remind me of everything I hated about being the man America thought they knew. She reminds me of everything that I miss about Lauren.

"In five, four, three, two…" The man behind the camera doesn't count the last number for fear of being heard on television. It is live, after all.

As Cooper introduces the show, I try to push thoughts of Lauren out of my mind and focus. If I'm going to do damage control, I need to stop pouting about her and think about winning over hearts and minds.

Hearts and minds. Because those missions have always worked out well for me.

"Welcome to the show," Cooper cuts into my thoughts and I sit up straighter in my chair. "The last time I saw you was when you were still a patient at the Walter Reed medical facility. You were learning to walk again with your new prosthetic leg. The only time I had ever met you before that was when you lost that leg, by saving my life."

"Thank you for having me on," I nod sharply. I don't want to let my mind get dragged back to that day right now. Not when I struggle so hard everyday to let it go.

"It looks like you've come a long way from the man I watched fight for each baby step back at Walter Reed. Would you say that you've fully adjusted to living your life with an amputation now?" He throws me an easy one, like a softball being gently tossed into the glove of a toddler.

"I believe I have. I live my life like every other American now. There's nothing that I feel like my leg holds me back from anymore. I've learned to run with my new blade, and get out everyday for a jog or some sprints. It feels like my life before I lost the leg, except for one thing," I look up at him.

"What's that?"

"I still haven't gotten back on my bike yet. "I need to do that next. I can't tell you how much I've missed riding." I feel myself relaxing a bit as our conversation bounces back and forth like a ping pong ball.

"If my memory still serves me right, I believe you had plans to come home from the war and go on a cross country tour on your motorcycle. Is that still in the cards?" The silver haired news anchor's eyes twinkle.

"You better believe it, I want to get my bike out of storage next week and take her out for some short trips before I go out to the coast."

"Of course you do," he smiles. "For those who aren't familiar with your story, I'd like to play the video of that conversation we had, and the footage we have of your heroic bravery in Afghanistan. I must warn our viewers: this video is very graphic and raw, as war tends to be. I strongly recommend that if there are any children in the room under the age of fourteen that they be sent out now." He gives his content advisory and then pauses, again, unblinking. I'm beginning to wonder if he even needs eyelids at all.

"Are we good?" He looks over my shoulder to the producer. The bald man watching a monitor in front of him gives him a thumbs up. "Ok, so the people watching this are going to see the footage we got in the desert. Then they'll cut back to us and I'll talk to you about what happened the other day, ok?" His eyebrows look like they're trying to furrow, but between the fillers and the makeup, there's no chance of that happening.

"Sounds good, thanks man."

A couple of crew members shuffle up beside us with a small table and a laptop. "As you can see, for the discussion about what happened here on the road, I'm going to play you a bit of the video. Everyone has seen it so there's no need to watch the entire thing. I think seventy million views is more than enough," he chuckles.

Seventy million views? That's how many people watched my melt down? The number feels too large, too abstract to even be embarrassed by. I can't imagine what a thousand people look like, let alone seventy.

I don't have time to really mull it over though, because the man behind the camera is signalling us again. "We're back on in five, four, three, two…"

Anderson looks straight into the lens, "Welcome back. I'm sitting down with Captain Mack Forrester, for those of you who were able to watch the entire footage that we just shared with you, it's easy to see how the nickname "Captain America" was given to you. The heroism that you displayed that day was nothing short of the acts of bravery you would expect to see in a movie about a superhero." His eyes break from the camera and focus back on me.

I try not to squirm at the comparison, "Uh, thanks."

"I for one would like to thank you for your service and for the unflinching courage you showed when we came under attack. It must have been a surprise to you when, after the other video of you on the highway earlier this week went viral, how many people quickly turned against you." He rubs his thumb and forefinger over the meat of his hand, "I was disgusted when I saw calls for your medals to be rescinded. How have you been dealing with the fallout of Captain America?"

I blink for a moment, just trying to stay in the moment. "To be honest," I clear my throat loudly, "that name has never sat easy with me. It's always made me feel like it doesn't honor the men I lost that day by comparing me to a Hollywood character. How do I feel about them being angry?" I look down at my missing leg, "I'm sorry that I let people down, but I'm much more concerned with how I made the man who I dragged out of his vehicle and his family feel. Those are real people, whose lives I affected, and for that I'm sorry."

"I think that's appropriate. However, it appears to me that this entire thing has been blown out of proportion. As the last video we shared just showed, you've been through more than most people will ever face. You're a true hero. You've sacrificed your own health and safety to save others. Now, because you experienced some road rage, people are demanding that you return your medals? I get road rage every week!" His unbiased reporting is getting buried under his emotions. "Everyone gets annoyed sometimes. I'm going to play a bit of the video showing the events that took place earlier in the week, in case there are some viewers at home who still haven't seen it." He leans forward and presses play on the already loaded video.

On the laptop monitor, the familiar footage plays. I've seen bits and pieces of this video on the different news stations all week. Usually about ten seconds worth is all I've gotten through before shutting it off. My entire body tingles as I watch myself beating on the window of the man's van. It's strange to see yourself do something that you have no memory of. Like watching footage of yourself blacked out at a frat party. Who is that guy? Without the memory connecting me to the event, it feels surreal.

We've now made it past the part that I usually see before scrambling for the remote. Now, I'm wrenching the door open and unbuckling the man's seat belt in a panic. My seat suddenly feels extremely uncomfortable, like I just can't find a way to sit in it that isn't pinching into my skin. Cooper leans over to shut the remaining footage off, when the person who taped this on their cellphone suddenly sweeps across the car and over to Lauren and Chris.

"No, wait, don't turn it off." I reach out and grab his hand.

I can feel Cooper's stare boring into me, but I can't tear my eyes off the screen. Chris tries to break free from Lauren's arms to run over to me, but her and Chelsea firmly grab him by the shoulders and keep him by their side. It's a good thing too, with the state of mind I was in, I don't know what I would've done if he tried to intervene.

My guts twist up tight and my chest squeezes as I watch the tears slide down his face before he buries his head against his mother. Lauren is screaming my name, sobs convulsing through her body, but I'm too busy climbing into the man's van to even know they're near me. I let go of Cooper's hand and he shuts off the computer.

"So, those are not the actions that one would expect from a highly decorated war veteran," Cooper continues, "but, it doesn't look like anything more complicated than a little outburst of road rage. After all, you were stuck in construction, weren't you?" He looks up at me imploring me to follow the bouncing ball and help him downplay this whole thing.

"No." My voice is flat and empty.

"No? You weren't in a construction zone?" He sounds betrayed.

"No, it wasn't road rage. I wasn't even driving. I think…" my voice cracks and I breathe in deep, I will not cry on national television.

I give myself a second, but I can't push the image of Chris trying to run after me, trying to help me…what would I have done to him? What have I already done to him? To Lauren? To my family. I fight the tears forming in the corners of my eyes.

"What happened that day wasn't road rage, Cooper," my confession finally slips out. "I've been having flashbacks of the war ever since I returned home. I'm back there every night fighting in my dreams, and I'm often transported back in the day when something sets me off. I, well, I think that people look at me and they see that I've learned to walk again, and they say 'oh, he's better. He's healed.'

But I haven't healed. Because I have scars on the inside that no one can see, and they keep splitting open. I'm not better just because I can walk again. Not when my mind is still fighting a war."

I take a deep breath and look straight into the camera, "I need help. I'm going to get professional help."

CHAPTER 39:

Year – 2014

Mack

With a long day of fishing behind us, we're settled around the campfire for the night. When I first looked into the Odyssey Project with Wounded Warriors, I wasn't completely sold on their program. It just seemed like a bit of wishful thinking that you go out camping and fishing with other war veterans for a week and somehow you get better.

Luckily when I sat down with the program coordinator, Jay, he set me straight on how it all works. This is only my first day, but I already feel that familiar bond that you have with your brothers in arms. There is an instant understanding and respect given to anyone who served their country. However, that bond is much deeper when you know you're with others who fought for it as well.

I stare into the fire, we all do, as Tim Baines wraps up his introduction. "So, that's why I'm here," he finishes up.

"Great, welcome to the group, Tim." His eyes travel over our faces, "Mack Forrester? Would you mind sharing why you signed up for this program and what you hope to get out of it?"

I guess I'm up. I feel like when a teacher used to call on me in class because it was my turn to read. My head snaps up and my eyes try to focus after staring into the flickering flames to look at Jay.

"Uh, yeah. Sure," I clear my throat and look around self-consciously. However, none of the other guys are looking at me. They're all zoned out like I was a couple of seconds ago. Listening, but hypnotized by the fire.

I relax a little, realizing that there's no spotlight on me right now. This isn't like when I was awarded the medal of honor by the president. Hell, it ain't even like sitting down with Cooper Sanders last month. These are my guys, we don't know each other yet, but our shared experiences are enough to bond us.

"When I got home from Afghanistan, I didn't have time to think about much. I was so doped up on painkillers and meds that I got the best sleep I'd had in years. But, once they cut back on the pills, I had time to think. I thought about the men I lost. How I let them and their families down. I was consumed with guilt and anger.

Honestly, there were days when I wanted to give up. There were a lot of days I asked God why he didn't just let me die over there too." My voice cracks and I have to fight a lump in my throat just to swallow. I've never really talked about those dark days. When living felt like a worse option than dying.

I breathe in deep and push myself to keep going. No one said this would be easy. But nothing worth doing is. "One day I was talking to a pastor who lost his arm over there on a different rotation, and he told me that God had a plan for me and it wasn't up to me to question it. It made me look at my recovery differently. I stopped feeling sorry for myself and put everything I had into healing. Into walking. Into making everyone believe I was the same guy I had always been."

I run my hand over my beard and look around the circle of men sitting around the fire. Some of them are nodding, others look lost in their own stories, but each of them still has their eyes on the crimson flames.

"And what happened?" Jay interrupts my thoughts and gently nudges me back on track.

"I think I did a great fucking job," I laugh. "You know, for a while there, I even had myself fooled." My smile fades as I lower my voice, "but then the flashbacks started." I look down into my hands, "that first one, it scared the shit out of me. It was intense," I blink back tears and look over at Jay. I need to look into a friendly face to keep me in the present.

"Did you know what it was?" He prods me on.

"No. Well, I knew it wasn't good. I'd seen enough movies about war and shit to know that much. You know, it's funny though, if someone else had told me they were going through the same thing I would've had no problem identifying it. I would point at them and say, 'oh, that's PTSD. You should go talk to someone, it's totally normal after what you've been through.' But I couldn't admit that shit to myself. I just couldn't."

"Why not?" Jay is asking me questions that make Cooper Sanders look like an amateur. I mull it over. Why couldn't I see it in myself?

"It wasn't because I didn't know. The flashbacks, they got worse. And then, so did the nightmares. I knew what was going on in the back of my head, but I didn't want to admit it. Honestly, I'm still uncomfortable." I rub my hands together and look back into the fire.

"You know," I continue, "if it was someone else, I would say there's nothing wrong with admitting you need help and all that. But, for me, it wasn't like that. It's like when I went to basic and they talked about PTSD in one of the classes. Even then, they give the whole 'there's no shame' speech, but there was something false about it. The tone they use, the eye rolls. It's like they have to teach it because it's a law or something, not because anyone really believes it."

"So, you felt ashamed. Do you still feel that way now?" Jay pushes me.

"Yeah. I guess I do. I can't help but feel like when you admit you have PTSD; those four letters hang around your neck in a neon sign that spells 'broken' to everyone else. You know?" I look around for validation. Guys in the circle are nodding silently.

"I just," my voice breaks, "I just spent so much time trying to fix everything. I wanted to somehow fix what happened over there. I wanted to fix my leg so no one would know by looking at me that it was fucked up. I wanted to fix everyone's lives that I messed up in one way or another. But, I couldn't fix myself. I couldn't make it go away..." tears stream down my cheeks and my throat feels like I swallowed a coal. "I couldn't fix it," I sob.

Tears fall down my cheeks and into my beard. For a few seconds the only sounds in the camp are the crackle of the burning fire and me crying.

"Thank you for sharing that," Jay finally softly speaks. "I think you're going to find that most of us in this group have felt or do feel that way too. You're not alone. This is only the first step in healing, but once you've gone through the entire program I think you'll find you're stronger for admitting you needed help," he explains gently.

"Thanks," I wipe the tears away with the back of my hand. My chest already feels like someone has removed a crushing rock from it. I'm still on my back, and my lungs need work, but I can already breathe just a little easier. "I already do."

CHAPTER 40:

Year - 2014

Lauren

I'm excited, I'm nervous … I think I might throw up! If Mack Forrester only knew the real effect he had on women.

It's been two, excruciatingly long months since I watched Mack finally confess that he needed help. Two months that I haven't been able to look into his eyes. Two months that I haven't been able to kiss his lips. Two months that I haven't been able to feel his rock hard cock fucking me.

I mean, a girl has needs too, damn it! Sixty days is a long time to go. Not that I'm counting or anything. Sixty-three and a half. See, I've barely even noticed.

That's not to say that we've been out of touch for two months. Instead, we've been talking on the phone and texting like a couple of teenagers. I haven't felt like such a love-struck dope, smiling down at my phone all the time since … well, since Mack and I were in high school. I guess some things never change.

"You look so good, Lauren," Chelsea reassures me as I squint at myself in the mirror for the billionth time.

"You don't think I'm wearing too much make-up?" I look at her past my reflection in the mirror.

"No, it's just the right amount. You're already a natural beauty, now it's just in high def," she smiles.

Mack is taking me out on a date tonight and from my dry mouth and nervous tummy, you'd think I'd never gone on one before in my life. Of course, him refusing to tell me where we're going or what he's got planned hasn't helped at all.

I give myself one last look in the mirror. Oh, who am I kidding, I'll be back here in five minutes to scrutinize again. Chelsea is right though; my make-up does look good. So does my manicure and my hair, and even though she doesn't know it, the wax job I got doesn't look bad either.

Just because she's my sister doesn't mean she needs to know every little detail.

I turn and look at her, the sparkle in her big brown eyes makes me wonder who's more excited? Her or me?

"I hope I'm not overdressed. Or underdressed," I look down at the black blouse and jeans I finally managed to settle on.

"You'll be fine! You look fine! Just relax, Lauren. You won't have any fun if you're just hyperventilating the whole time. You're gonna have a great night, ok? And you know you don't have to worry about Chris, he's got the world's best aunt to look after him, so chill, will ya?"

I open my mouth to spill a laundry list of more worries and concerns, but my voice is drowned out.

Vroom-tick-tick-tick!

What the hell was that?

Chelsea, Chris and I all rush over to the living room window and see Mack pop out the kickstand on his motorcycle and tilt it onto the support as he steps off. I'd be scared that he showed up on his bike, if a larger part of me wasn't aching with desire just from watching him park it.

"Whoa," Chris gives his approval and my sister and I watch Mack remove his helmet and walk toward the door.

It feels like a scene from a movie. Probably a James Bond movie, because there's just one teensy, minor detail that Mack didn't fill me in on. Where ever he's taking me tonight, he's taking me there wearing a tuxedo.

I'm painfully underdressed, that much is clear, but I can't scrape two shits together about it right now. Not when Mack "Captain

America" Forrester shows up in some sexy man-lingerie on the back of a Harley.

I rush over to the door and yank it open with all of the patience of a kid opening gifts on Christmas.

"Mack!" I throw my arms around him as soon as he steps through the door. His arms wrap around my waist and he easily lifts me from my feet and swirls me around.

For a moment, my mind flashes back to when we were kids and he talked me into being spun around on the merry-go-round at our park. I remember clearly how I clung onto those bars for dear life as Mack spun me around in nauseating circles until my façade of bravery broke down and I screamed his name in pure terror. In an instant, he thrust himself up onto the spinning cyclone from hell and grabbed onto my arms. "Don't let go of me," I cried desperately.

"Never." It was a one-word sentence, a statement and a promise spun into one.

Mack places me on my tipsy feet and gives me a quick kiss on the tip of my nose.

"Hey Mack!" Chris leaps over to him.

"My man!" Mack high fives him enthusiastically.

Our son could compete with the sun right now for who's shining brightest.

"Mack, nice to see you again," Chelsea smiles at him.

"Hey, lady! Thanks for helping me out," he nods over at her and I know I don't have a cool superhero nickname but my Spidey sense starts tingling. Helping him with what?

"What are you wearing," I interrupt their meaningful looks. "I'm not dressed for where we're going if you're wearing a tux!" I look down over the outfit I painfully picked out, rejected, tried back on, and finally settled on.

"Don't worry about that!" Chelsea interrupts before I have a chance to fully get immersed in Mack's hypnotizing stare. "Come with me, I've got you something to wear," she slides up beside me and grabs my hand.

She quickly pulls me up the stairs before I have a chance to process much of what's happening let alone protest over it. I look down over my shoulder as my feet automatically follow my sister and I see Chris and Mack talking like two old friends at a party.

It's hard to be overly concerned with whatever the hell is going on right now when my Mom heart is overflowing with joy.

Chelsea leads me back down to my bedroom and lets go of my hand, leaving me to fend for myself by the door while she raids my closet. What the hell is she doing?

Quickly, she slides hanger after hanger forward until she finds whatever she's looking for. She pulls a floor length, purple gown from behind my work clothes and tosses it on the bed.

"Put this on," she smiles.

"Where did that come from?" I peer past her into my magical closet making amazing, elegant ball gowns appear. Is there a door to Narnia back there too?

"I hid it in there," she looks entirely too proud of herself with her chest puffed out and her eyes twinkling.

"Oh, you did, huh?"

"Yeah, and I know it's a perfect fit cause I got your measurements from your other clothes. Well, from the ones you actually wear," she laughs at her jab about my collection of clothes I'll never fit into again.

I look at the lavender dress on my bed and then back to my sister. I know she's got my best interest at heart, so I won't question her… not yet anyway.

Instead, I slip out of the clothes I agonized over and put the dress on. "Can you zip me up, please?" I look over my shoulder at her.

"Sure." She helps me close the back as I admire how the light purple hue of the dress plays off of my skin tone. I look good, even if I do say so myself.

"Where's Mack taking me? Why are we dressing up like this?" I turn and confront Chelsea once I feel the zipper reach the top.

"Nope. I'll never tell you," she sing-songs. Like she's a five-year-old version of herself taunting the three-year-old version of myself.

She clamps down on my hand and practically drags me out of the bedroom, back down the hall and to the stairs.

"Oh, mom! You look like a princess!" Chris exclaims and almost immediately bashfully looks at his feet, like he's ashamed of his declaration. It's probably incredibly uncool to say that to your mom. It might be uncool, but I'd be lying if I said it didn't make my week.

"He's not wrong, you know," Mack's eyes glide over me from head to toe. "You look amazing, but I don't think you look like a princess," he looks up at me after sweeping his eyes down my body all the way to my bare feet.

"Oh, no?" I pout.

"No. You don't look like a princess, because you're no princess. You're my queen." He grabs my hand and twirls me around in a small circle. I spin around with my eyes closed and enjoy the way the dress feels as it billows out around my legs.

I do feel like a queen. His queen. Wait, a minute. This queen doesn't have any shoes to wear with this dress.

"My feet!" I stop on a dime and look down at my toes woefully.

"Got it covered," Chelsea smiles.

"Come over here," Mack walks me back to my couch and I sit as soon as my legs touch the seat.

Chelsea rummages in the back of my coat closet and pulls out a shoe box. "Got it!"

Seriously? Is my whole house full of hidden Easter eggs for this date?

She drops the box beside Mack, who is kneeling at my feet. He opens the lid and I watch with my breath held as he pulls out the first velvet crushed high heel shoe. The heel must be six inches long. I'm going to officially break my neck tonight, that much is apparent. I look up at Chelsea, her smug smile is practically popping off her face. I'm 100% certain that these shoes were her brainchild.

Make that 1000%

Mack holds it in his hand, smirking up at me. "Let's see if the shoe fits," he teases me, sliding it onto my foot.

It does fit. Perfectly.

He puts the other one on me and I can't help but wonder if I'm about to get whisked away in a pumpkin carriage. Remembering that there's a motorcycle in the driveway waiting for me makes my stomach turn cold.

"A perfect fit." Mack stands back up and helps me off the couch. In these heels, I can use all the help I can get.

Teetering on the brink of disaster I look down at our son, who is beaming his radiant smile up at us. "Ok, we're going to head out now, Chris. Please promise me that you'll be good for your aunt?"

"I promise!" He crosses his heart, reminding me of his father only a few months back making me a similar promise in the backyard.

"I can't promise I'll have her back by midnight," Mack winks at Chelsea.

"Don't rush back, we're good," she cheerfully answers. "Have fun you two!"

I follow Mack out the front door over to the bike and wonder how this is going to work, exactly.

"Here, we're not going that far, but I want you to wear the helmet," he hands it to me.

"Uh, ok." I grab it from him and look down at it.

"Mack! Lauren! Wait!" Chelsea yells from the front step dramatically. She's holding something in her hands and runs over to us in her bare feet.

"You almost forgot this," she stuffs the white cardboard box into Mack's hands and then gives me a meaningful look before disappearing back inside the house.

"What's that?" I look down into Mack's hands and wait for him to pop the lid on this mystery.

"It's for you," he opens the box and inside is a corsage. Violet and white roses are twisted up with some babies' breath. He holds it over my wrist.

"Lauren, will you do me the honor of going to the prom with me tonight?" He peers into my face with his crystal blue eyes and I don't even want to question the insanity. I just want to hand over my ticket and take the ride with Mack into the madness he's clearly planned out for us.

"Yes." I hold out my wrist for him. "Yes, I will."

CHAPTER 41:

Year - 2014

Lauren

Mack pulls up to the Colorado Golf Club and brings his motorcycle to a stop. I thought seeing him on the back of the Harley was hot, it was practically orgasmic to be on there with him. I never realized that I could be so terrified and turned on at the same time.

He helps me down from the seat and I quickly smooth out the bunched up dress that I transformed into a makeshift pair of pants between my legs. I pop the helmet off my head and hope that it hasn't messed up my hair too badly.

"You look stunning," Mack murmurs, pulling me close. My self-consciousness evaporates as he wraps his strong arms around me. It's impossible to feel insecure when a man like Mack Forrester looks at you like that. His lips cover mine with a tender kiss. Prickles of desire cover my skin as I melt into his tight embrace.

I know that Mack put a lot of thought and time into tonight, that's already clear. However, I'm just kinda wishing he'd saved himself the trouble and just booked us a hotel instead.

Five minutes without oxygen would be easier than two months without Mack. Every cell in my body *craves* him.

Needs him.

Screams his name.

He releases my lips from his tantalizing kiss and my eyelids flutter back open. "Are you ready?" His eyes sparkle.

"Since you still haven't told me what you've got cooked up in there, I guess I'm as ready as I'll ever be." My lips twitch up into a smile and betrays my complaining. He knows full well that I'm loving this.

"All will be revealed soon," he teases me dramatically and holds out his arm to me. I cling onto it for dear life. Ok, maybe not for the sake of my life, but certainly for the sake of my ankles.

Damn Chelsea and her love of stilettos. I swear she must have worked the pole in another life. If it was in this one, I don't wanna know.

Safe on Mack's arm, I let him guide me to the door I haven't stepped through for a decade. I blink my eyes to adjust to the darkened room we step into.

"Oh, Mack!"

It's the only words I can squeak out. I feel like we just walked into a dream. From the ceiling are the same clusters of teal, silver and white balloons, hanging like magical clouds. Draped over the walls is the same silky fabric that I remember from our prom night. Right down to the streamers and the "Congratulations to the Class of 2004!" sign hanging on the back wall, everything looks the same.

There are three ways this could have happened. This country club may have been sporting this décor for ten years. I've stepped into a time warp. Or, Mack has spent countless hours recreating every detail of our last night together before both our lives changed forever.

I manage to close my mouth and smile at the most incredible man I've ever known. "It's amazing, Mack!" I lean my head against his arm and look over all the hard work and thought he's put into making this re-imagined prom.

"This is just a room. You, on the other hand, now that's what I call amazing," he guides me to the only table and chairs set up across the room.

Being every bit the prince charming that I wished for ten years ago, he pulls my seat out and helps me tuck into the table. I've gotta admit, I'm enjoying the princess treatment. I just hope Mack isn't such a gentleman later. When I rip that tux off his hard body and fuck his brains out.

Mack takes his seat across from me and reaches for my hand across the table. "I missed you," his eyes search my face. I'm sure he can read every emotion on my face like words in a book.

"I missed you too. So much. I know it was for the best and that you needed that time to work on everything, but I'd be lying if I said it wasn't hard," my eyes mist over.

"Hey, don't cry. I'm here now," he traces his thumb along my bottom lid and gathers the tears threatening to ruin my makeup.

"It was hard for me too," his blue eyes stare into mine earnestly. "But, now I know I can give you all of me, not just fragments left over from the war. I'm not saying I'm perfect. I mean, I'm pretty close, obviously," he teases me.

"You are." I know he's kidding around, but I'm not.

Mack smiles. "Thank you. Too bad I didn't record that. It would've been perfect for six months from now when you're giving me a hard time about leaving the toilet seat up or something."

The reference doesn't escape me. My heart soars as I digest his words. He wasn't us to live together? Before I can respond, a waiter interrupts our chat with a bottle of champagne and two glasses on a tray.

"May I start your evening with a drink?" He offers.

"Yes, thank you," Mack nods. The man places the glasses between us and then reaches for the bottle.

"You can just leave the bottle with us. We have a lot to celebrate," Mack grins.

Our server doesn't argue; he simply places it between us. "Your dinner will be ready shortly," he informs Mack before disappearing back over my shoulder.

I shouldn't be surprised that Mack also had our prom for two catered, but I am. Just like the man who just walked across the floor to the set up the turn tables in the back corner shouldn't surprise me either, but here we are.

Soft music floods the sound system and Mack pours each of us a glass of the bubbly champagne. He lifts his glass in a toast, and I imitate him, eager to hear what he has to say.

"Lauren, you look just as beautiful tonight as you did a decade ago. I was the luckiest man at our prom then, and tonight you've made me the luckiest man in the world tonight by being on my arm."

"Thank you," I don't know what else to say, Mack's never been one for flowery speeches, but I guess he's just full of surprises tonight.

"No, thank you." He answers. "I figured that there was no better place to ask for a mulligan than at a golf club, so…"

"A mulligan?" I interrupt. I'm not sure what he's talking about.

"Yeah, it's a golf term. It's for a do over? You've never heard that before?" His eyes crinkle at the corners, "look, all you need to know is that besides being incredibly handsome, I'm also very witty," he laughs.

"And humble, too," I tease him.

"Yes, humble as fuck," he grins. There's my old Mack. "Anyway, to new beginnings," he raises his glass higher and I raise mine.

The first sip of the champagne is heaven; the tiny bubbles tickle my lips but feel smooth on my tongue.

Mack empties his glass in one long gulp, then takes a deep breath. "Lauren?"

"Yeah?"

"Will you dance with me?"

My ears are ringing with shock. Never in my entire life has Mack danced with me. Never. No matter how much I've pleaded, or whined, or threatened him with teenaged angst. He's never given in.

"Of course," I barely breathe the words, like they're caught in my throat.

He stands up and holds his hand out to me, and I steady myself with his strength and follow him to the dance floor. The music suddenly changes to Coldplay.

Come up to meet you, tell you I'm sorry
You don't know how lovely you are
I had to find you
Tell you I need you
Tell you I set you apart
Tell me your secrets
And ask me your questions
Oh, let's go back to the start

Perfect. Absolutely perfect song with my absolutely perfect man. This couldn't possibly get any better. Mack holds my waist and dances with all of the grace of a middle school boy, but it's so charming, I just love him even more for his lack of skill.

I lean my head against his chest and breathe him in. "Thank you for this Mack. For all of this. I, well, I don't even know what to say except that it's magical."

Tell me you love me
Come back and haunt me
Oh, and I rush to the start
Running in circles
Chasing our tails
Coming back as we are

"That's appropriate," he chuckles and I look up at him.

"Why's that?"

"Didn't our first prom have a princess theme or something?" He looks down at me.

"Yeah, well, the theme was fairy tales. So, yeah, it's fitting that tonight is magical," I smile back.

"Well, what's a fairy tale without a happy ending?" Mack stops our dance and looks me straight in the eyes. I think he's going to kiss me, my lips are already pushed up into a pout and instead he slides down onto his good leg, kneeling before me.

He lets go of my hand and reaches into his tuxedo jacket, pulling out the familiar velvet box that held the engagement ring he gave me on the Ferris wheel. It isn't just familiar because of his proposal. It's because ever since he walked out of my car at the police station that ring has been sitting on my bedside table in that very box.

"How did you get that?" I don't mean to accuse him; I'm just surprised to see it back in his hand.

He lifts the lid, and sure enough, it's the same ring. "Chelsea snuck it into my pocket before we left," he smiles up at me, his eyes twinkling.

Of course she did. She's so stealthy.

"Lauren, will you give me the chance to start over with you? To fulfill the destiny, I've known was mine since I was six years old? Will you become my wife?"

In my mind, I can still see his round face at six. His sweet smile that transformed into his irresistible smirk over the years. "Yes, of course I will. Yes!" I hold out my trembling hand and Mack slips the ring back into place on my finger. I know in my heart that it will never be taken off again. What Mack and I have can never be destroyed. Fate has just pushed us back where we always belonged. In each other's arms.

Mack stands back up and wraps his arms around me, his lips softly opening mine until our tongues finish this dance for us. In each other's arms. It's where we've always been, it's where we'll always be. Until death do us part.

Nobody said it was easy
Oh, it's such a shame for us to part
Nobody said it was easy

No one ever said it would be so hard
I'm going back to the start.

EPILOGUE
Lauren

"What a gorgeous day, "I look up at the dark blue sky and breathe in a lungful of air that somehow feels cleaner. Like it always does in September.

"You wanna talk about gorgeous? Look at you two," Mack leans over and kisses me on the cheek and then over further to kiss our ten month-old daughter, Honor, on her button nose.

Honor giggles and grabs her daddy's face with both hands and slobbers with an open mouth down the side of his beard. She hasn't quite perfected the art of kissing yet.

Mack laughs and wipes the baby drool off with the back of his arm.

"Can I hold her?" Chris interrupts.

I've gotta admit, I was nervous when I first learned I was pregnant with Honor. The age gap between her and Chris seemed too insurmountable for them to ever be close. I'm so happy that my fears were unfounded. Her big brother might be a lot older than her, but their bond couldn't be better. He absolutely adores his baby sister. If anything, it seems like the age gap has worked to his benefit. He's had eleven years of being an only child and soaking up all the attention, he seems relieved to share the limelight with someone new. We'll see how that goes once the infamous teen years hit, but right now, I'm just enjoying living in the moment.

"Sure, bud. You can hold her." I carefully move Honor into my son's arms. She's still not walking yet, but she's so squirmy she can be difficult to hang onto. Luckily, today she's feeling pretty snuggly, so she tucks her head in against Chris's chest and shows off her new teeth in a tiny grin. With her mocha skin and large brown eyes, she's already breaking all the baby boy's hearts.

"Guys! Hey! Look, you're on the kiss cam!" Chelsea excitedly points to the giant screen across the stadium. I look over to where her finger is waving and, sure enough, Mack and I are smiling at ourselves from across the field.

"Well, we wouldn't want to let them down, now would we?" Mack wraps his arms around me tight. Our lips find each other, tenderly at first, but like every kiss with Mack, the spark of passion quickly ignites and burns like a sparkler in a child's hand on July 4th.

Around us, I can hear clapping and whooping for our lip lock. However, above all the commotion I can hear Chris groaning.

"Mom! You're embarrassing me!"

I pull away from Mack and save my son the public humiliation of his parent's love.

"Thanks for letting us know about the camera, Chelsea," I look over Mack to her but she doesn't hear me. Now that the intermission is over, she's completely immersed back into the game. My sister the super fan. I can't help but wonder if she would be so invested in the game if Cameron Armstrong wasn't the quarterback on the field right now.

My money is on no.

"Are you nervous about being the old man on campus?" I nudge Mack in the ribs.

Ever since Mack got a job as an outreach coordinator with the Wounded Warrior Project, he's been thinking about going back to school. He loves going around to the military hospitals, talking to other veterans, and their families. And they love him. With a story as public as Mack's has been, they know they're getting the real deal when he talks to them. Now he's enrolled here, at the University of Colorado, part time so he can take some psychology courses. I don't think he's ever going to chase after a psych degree, but he's dedicated to learning as much as he can so he can help his men.

"I know you can't be talking about me," Mack teases. "Cause this guy," he points his thumbs at his chest, "is in the prime of his life. Are you worried about your husband being the big man on campus?" He turns my question around on me.

I'm not. It isn't because Mack isn't sexy, or funny, or doesn't still have little bimbos that flirt with him from time to time, because all of that is true. It's because I know he loves me. Only me. Always me.

"Should I be?" I smile up at him, just because I know I have nothing to worry about doesn't mean I don't like to hear it from him, too.

"Of course not! You know that," he throws his arm around my shoulders and gives me a squeeze.

"Yeah, I do." I lean my head against his shoulder and breathe him in. Even after sleeping next to this man for two years, I still think there's no greater aphrodisiac than his scent.

"Did you see that?" Chelsea screams and points to the field. It's over! They slaughtered that game." She yells excitedly.

I didn't really see it, with Mack and my beautiful children distracting me, this game was little more than background noise on a perfect day. Still, I appreciate that Cameron got us these seats. Now that we've sat this close to the field twice, it's spoiled me. I could never sit in the cheap seats for an entire game again.

Mack's arm slides off my shoulders and he jumps to his feet as the players clear the field. I stand up next to him and take Honor back into my arms, giving her a kiss on her chubby cheek.

People around us start to shuffle around and gather their things to leave, but Mack doesn't move. I have a feeling I know why.

Sure enough, I see Cameron pull off his helmet and slowly jog over to us. It's like I'm having a flashback to two years ago, but I have a feeling that this time he's not coming over to talk to Chris.

I glance over a Chelsea and she's running her hands over her hair nervously. I swear these two are like a couple of kids admiring each other across the cafeteria at lunch, but never saying 'hi' to each other. It's too bad that king quarterback Armstrong has been too busy indulging in his own fan club for the past two years. I really thought him and Chelsea would've at least gone on a date by now. I'm not sure who's more disappointed that it never happened for them, me or her.

No, I'm kidding. It's her. *Definitely* her.

"Hey man, great start to the season! You're killing it out there," Mack shakes Cameron's hand.

"Thanks, gotta shine for all those scouts, right? Apparently college doesn't go on forever. Eventually they hand you a piece of paper and ask you to leave campus." He smiles over at Chelsea.

I look at my sister and her grin could stop traffic. Subtle. Real subtle.

"Awesome game, Armstrong," Chris holds out his hand confidently. My heart swells with pride. He's quite a bit taller since he got a tour of this stadium a couple years back. I'm so grateful for Mack and Cameron talking to him and helping him get the closure he so desperately needed.

"Hey man, long time no see," Cameron shakes his hand. "Did you ever make it onto the team?" He looks at my son and I can see that Chris is flattered that the quarterback remembered his goals.

"I did. I'm a running back on the school team," he puffs his chest out proudly. He has every reason to be proud. After I got Chris a fresh start in a new school district, you never would have known he had been the same kid who had been expelled. He studied hard and got on the honor roll and his report cards went from a day we both dreaded in the year to glowing.

"Great job, man. Keep working on it and maybe you'll be the one catching a scout's eye." Cameron claps his hand on Chris's arm.

"Well, you're really making a name for yourself here," Chelsea interrupts. "I bet you'll get picked up the draft first," she smiles.

"I'd like to think that's true. But I thought I made a name for myself in high school too, but you don't remember me from back then do ya?" He puts her on the spot.

Chelsea fidgets a little and furrows her eyebrows together. "Uh, yeah, sure I do." The lie is so painfully obvious; it makes me grimace.

"Yeah, it sounds like I made a real impression," Cameron teases her. "I'll tell you what, how about you give me your number and I'll take you out next Friday. This time I'll make sure you never forget me," his eyes narrow and his voice drops.

"I'd like that," Chelsea answers. I think we have a winner for understatement of the year.

As my sister types her digits into Cameron's phone, I look up at Mack. I'm so happy that I've already found my man. The father of my children. My soulmate. My forever.

"Let's give these two some space," I whisper up at him. He looks down at me with his crystal blue eyes and for the tenth time today I remember how lucky I am. How lucky we are.

"Sounds good. And then when I get you home, I think we should go find some space of our own. I have plans for you," he murmurs.

"I'd like that," I steal the understatement of the year award from my sister in three small words.

"Chelsea, we'll meet you in the car, ok? I want to get Honor's stuff packed up. No rush though, ok?" I look over at my sister.

"Sure," she answers without taking her eyes off Cameron Armstrong. I suppose it's not hard to see why, with his sandy brown hair and dark blue eyes, he's got a boyish charm about him that he never lost after high school. It's nice to see that he's looking at her with the same degree of desire tattooed across his face.

As we leave them to chat, I look over my family. My son, growing up into a wonderful young man. My daughter, whose whole life is open to possibilities. My husband, who is helping me write the chapters of my life, one page at a time. I gaze at them and know how my story is going to end.

When I glance back over my shoulder to Chelsea and Cameron, I can't help but wonder if their story is just beginning.

THANK YOU!

Thank you for reading my first novel. As a recently retired military veteran, this story was important to me. After growing up in a military family and serving for twelve years myself, I've watched too many suffer from PTSD.

I wanted to tell a story about the scars that go unseen in our wounded and bring their struggle to light. I appreciate you giving my first book a chance.

Made in the USA
Lexington, KY
24 January 2017